The Sundering

Novella #2 in THE DEER KING Series

I0620928

Ben Spencer

ISBN-13: 9781732038011 (Paperback)

KNOCK-KNEE BOOKS

About the Author

Ben Spencer lives in Concord, NC, with his wife and daughter. He is the author of THE DEER KING, an epic fantasy series of novellas. Please visit benspencerwrites.com and sign up to follow his blog for information on new THE DEER KING releases. You can also follow Ben on twitter at @RBenSpen.

For Mom

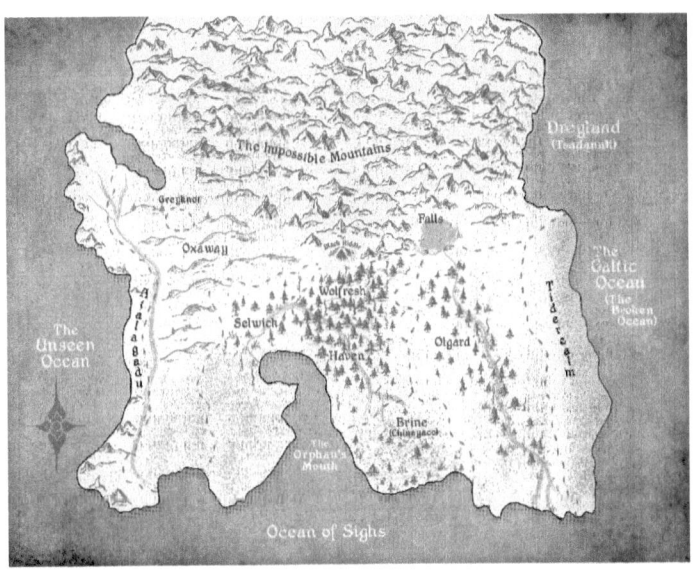

Dregland
(Tsadanuk)

The Impossible Mountains

Gregknor

Oxawall

Falls

The Baltic Ocean
(The Broken Ocean)

Wolfrest

Selwich

Olgard

The Unseen Ocean

Alalabau

Haven

Tidestream

Brine
(Chimigaco)

The Orphan's Mouth

Ocean of Sighs

1

199 A.D. (After Drey)

Boselmia knew that her brother was dead. She had felt it in her sawdust bones, in her runny blood, in the aching cavities plaguing her mouth. But still she waited. For seven days, three more than it should have taken him to return. She sat on the wicker chair in the depths of the fallen dew oak and hummed songs of the blackest death, the only activity that gave her solace. When the boy-god approached, she sent him scurrying with threats in a language he understood but would only sometimes speak. She knew that he was lovesick for the Stoneman's daughter, and that he needed guidance, but at the moment giving direction, let alone affection, was beyond her. She had been the *Fecheholo* for so long that sometimes it felt that she had forgotten what it was like to be human.

She supposed that what she was really trying to do was mourn.

On the evening of the seventh day, she made her peace with Prala's passing. She exited the dew oak and called to the boy-god in the oldest tongue, a tongue that predated even the Jindois people, a tongue so wise, it didn't know its own name. He approached with caution, wary of her recent bad temper.

"We have to leave," she said to the boy, continuing in the old tongue. She had learned the old tongue years ago, when she was deep inside the Black Riddle and on the verge of losing her mind. Her mother, Maisa—the *Fecheholo* at the time—had experienced the same trials inside the Black Riddle, only Maisa managed to learn more of the language than Boselmia, without nearly going insane. This memory and many others were constant reminders to Boselmia that she was a pale approximation of the Raven Queen her mother had been.

"Why?" the boy asked. His eyes twitched to *iiwase*, and for a moment Boselmia thought she saw her little brother, the fourth Deer King, launching himself at the Harrish hero Brigand Potter,

the instant before Potter's musket ended his life. She brushed aside the vision.

"So that you may live," she answered.

He stared at her. Holding up under the Deer King's stare was a difficult thing—it felt like being exposed to a violent storm—but she was the *Fecheholo*, so she didn't flinch. His gaze lasted a full minute, until, in the Deer King's quintessential way, his eyes simply wandered away, signaling acceptance. No further words were necessary. She went back inside the fallen dew oak to gather her things.

When she emerged from the tree for the second time, several of the villagers were waiting for her. The pot-bellied minor chieftain, Hasol, was among them, a nervous look about him; Boselmia guessed that he had been nominated to speak to her. She reached into the folds of her black-feathered cloak and fished out a *bittirinu* while he worked up the nerve. Seeing the *bittirinu*, an enterprising young girl caught her eye and ran off to light a spill. While she waited, Boselmia hocked a gob of spit in her paper-dry mouth and licked the ends of the hush-hush leaf, her tongue retrieving flecks of tobacco. The taste of it made her impatient for the smoke. She looked past Hasol, searching for the girl.

"Revered *Fecheholo*," Hasol at last began. "I have grievous news. We would have told you earlier, but you have been holed up in the dew oak for days, and no one wanted to disturb…"

The Raven Queen laughed, jarring Hasol into silence. The girl, fast as a scalded hare, was already racing back, a lick of flame on the end of a splinter of wood. Boselmia broke off her cachinnation and caught Hasol's eye.

"Go on, fat man. You were on the verge of telling me that my brother Prala had died."

The girl broke into the semicircle of villagers while Hasol choked on a reply. The girl held the splinter of wood aloft like a prized scalp. Boselmia did her the honor of leaning forward so that the girl could bring the flame to Boselmia's lips. When she sucked in the smoke from the *bittirinu*, it tasted like bliss.

"You already know?" Hasol finally managed.

"Of course I know, you upright toad. He should have returned three days ago. But he hasn't. So he's dead."

She enjoyed an extended drag of the *bittirinu* while Hasol collected himself once more. She had the same conflicted feelings for Hasol that she had for this whole village full of fanatics—she begrudged him, and them, for the simplicity of their faith. She had always thought it unfair: those who worshipped her and the *Dachahelu* simply had to believe, while she and the Deer King had to do the actual labor of bringing the prophecies to fruition. *You should all take turns playing the deity sometime,* she thought, casting withering looks at the villagers. *You might not be so devout if it required believing in yourself.*

She had always had a streak of self-loathing unbecoming of a god.

"Then we remain in possession of only one of Doido's pebbles?" Hasol asked.

Boselmia summoned a great store of acerbity. "Unless my dead brother crawled up your asshole and stuck the other one there before perishing, then yes, that appears to be the case."

Hasol winced, but not to the degree Boselmia would have liked: his tolerance for abuse seemed to be increasing the longer they talked. Boselmia noted the expectant expressions on the villagers' faces: they were still waiting on Hasol to ask the paramount questions. She could already guess at the queries forming on his tongue, and she resented them before they were even asked. Only the weak asked questions to which they already knew the answer.

At last he found his voice. "Does this mean the Harrish are coming?" She tried to frighten him away from a follow-up question by staring daggers at him while puffing on the *bittirinu,* but he powered ahead. "And, if they do, do you intend to leave with the *Dachahelu*?"

She ground her rotting back molars, biting the end of the *bittirinu* in the process. *No surprise they're worried that I'll leave with the boy. Without him to stir them into a crazed warlike state, they're nothing but weak, lily-livered cowards waiting for the day the Harrish run out of living space and march north.*

"Of course the Harrish are coming," she answered. "They've been coming for nearly two hundred years."

"Please, *Fecheholo.* Be direct. Do you believe that they'll seek out Prala's village? Our…village?"

3

"Most likely."

"But no one has broken the Accord! Not technically, at least…the priest escaped from here with his life and the stone…but now that the priest is dead and the stone is missing, they blame us…only Prala is dead, so it wasn't him who took it…"

Boselmia's heart stutter-stopped. Had she heard him correctly? "What do you mean, Doido's pebble is missing? The Havenese have it, don't they?"

Hasol looked at her in confusion. "I'm sorry, *Fecheholo*. You knew of your brother's death, so I thought you knew…the Havenese claim a Massaporan woman traveling with Prala stole it, and returned it to Wolfresh, to…*Jaironim*."

Her mind scrambled for an explanation. *A Massaporan woman?* Shocking as the news of the missing stone was, the explanation that a Massaporan woman had stolen the stone didn't add up. The idea that Prala would have brought another Massaporan with him into Haven was ludicrous—it was too dangerous, and besides, he would have discussed the matter with Boselmia before doing so. Then it dawned on her. *Some Havenese fool wants to start a war, so they've stolen the stone and conjured a Massaporan woman from thin air to play the thief.*

Hasol continued prattling. "*Fecheholo*? Please don't take the boy from us. Not if the Harrish are coming."

Lost in the rat's nest of her thoughts, she had almost forgotten Hasol. She glared at the fat chieftain and then at the other villagers, all of whom were straining to listen. *Helpless fools,* she thought. Even the girl who had brought her the splinter of fire looked lost, the enterprising spark that had spurred her to fetch the spill of wood now missing as she, like the rest, waited for Boselmia to inform her of her fate.

Boselmia felt a stirring within, the dark magic—or *jwonatuwe* —of the Black Riddle coming to life. The magic was always present in her blood, but there were times when it called to her with a disturbing intensity, begging to be unleashed. She stepped forward and, disregarding the terror in Hasol's eyes, placed her frail and bony hand upon his arm. She whispered an unintelligible word and his body went rigid. Unable to move, he became an instrument of her command. The other villagers did nothing to stop her; she was a higher power, and they had long ago accepted that they were slaves to higher powers.

"Listen to me, you weak and neutered dog. You trembling cockroach. You scared shitless little fat man. One day, when the *Dachahelu* is grown, he will slay our enemies by the tens of thousands. But that day is not today. And if I have to sacrifice one village so that we may prolong the boy's life in the hopes of reaching that day, so be it."

She should have released Hasol then. But she didn't. She felt the *jwonatuwe* coursing through her like a dark current, guiding her toward some unknown end. In retrospect, it felt like her decision, but at that moment it was no decision at all, only a happening, her body the conduit of a faraway god that it thrilled her to please. She brought Hasol to his knees, and as she did, a stain spread across his crotch, his bladder the only part of him not under her control. She muttered the word again and again. The meaning of the word evaded her conscious mind like a shiny, slippery fish, but it didn't matter, she knew what the word entailed. When Hasol started to convulse, she said the word even faster, until he collapsed on the ground. She didn't stop even after death had plucked him. When at last she came back into herself, she couldn't say how long she had continued chanting over his corpse.

She looked up, her power spent. The villagers were staring at her with the stares of the damned.

"You will stay here, and, if need be, you will die, so that your *Dachahelu* may live."

They said not a word, though their expressions spoke multitudes. She knew what they wanted. They wanted a glorious death, fighting alongside their god, touched with *iiwase*. But she didn't give a damn what they wanted. History had taught her that: if the Massaporan people had their way, the whole of the Massaporan race would either be enslaved or dead in the dust, and their gods lost to time. But she was a god, which meant she had to make decisions on behalf of the greater good. And she certainly wasn't going to let the lives of a few wretched zealots keep her from safeguarding the god they proclaimed to serve.

She stepped around Hasol's lifeless form. As she did, a wicked smile formed on her lips. The perfect verse from the *Showanai Hiip,* or The Broken Truth, materialized in her mind. She offered it to the villagers as a comfort.

"Failing this," she said, quoting the oral history, *"death is a doorway."*

2

140 A.D.

When she was a child, Boselmia's mother spoke the language of war to her the way that other mothers spoke sweet nothings to their children. She spoke it with a matter-of-factness that dulled its sharp edges, and she spoke it at moments so unforgettable that Boselmia couldn't help but retain the message. For example: when Maisa returned after the massacre of the Massaporan people at the Yipikurri River, and gave birth to the fourth Deer King, with Boselmia assisting as midwife.

"They make better butchers than we do. They have better weapons, and they have forged an alliance with death. I thought, as in the days of your namesakes, we might strike a blow that would halt our enemies' advance, but the Harrish are not like the Torquec. They have made slaves of our old enemies, and they will make corpses of us."

Maisa's voice was calm, but her eyes were wild. She always had a touch of the feral about her, but now, only hours removed from battle and on the verge of giving birth, she looked positively primal: her face was streaked with blood, her black hair was tempest-tossed, and her body was battle taut, attuned to the ongoing struggle.

Boselmia, unnerved by all that was occurring, tried to focus on the task at hand: she prepped dried strips of buckskin and a jar of rapeseed oil, and she cleaned the umbilical knife with grain alcohol, but even these simple tasks proved difficult with the noises filtering in from outside: in the village there was a wide range of sorrowful sounds, from the wailing of the injured to the weeping of the mournful to the despondent cries of those who had lost all hope, which made up the majority.

These weren't the only distractions. Boselmia kept waiting for her mother to explain where her father was. Before the battle, Maisa had claimed that Waisporek—Boselmia's father—was the Deer King born anew, and would lead the Massaporan people to victory. But now the battle was lost, and Waisporek was nowhere to be found.

"Where is father?" Boselmia asked, no longer able to contain herself. "You said that he was the *Dachahelu*. You said that he would lead our people to a great victory."

Maisa continued as if she hadn't heard her. "They will kill all of us, Boselmia, including you. They will tear this child from my womb and they will slit your throat and they will stick a sword through my gut, and with our deaths, the Massaporan people will be no more."

Boselmia felt hot tears of frustration welling up. She already knew in her heart that her father had died in battle, but she needed to hear it from her mother's lips to accept that it was true. Maisa had always treated Waisporek less as a husband than as a deity she was fashioning from clay, but to Boselmia, he was the one person who understood that she was more than the *Fecheholo's* daughter. She had always loved Waisporek because he loved her as a human, and not as the god her mother was preparing her to one day become.

Maisa was standing in the center of the room. Her ever-present cloak of raven feathers was bunched around her shoulders, but she was naked from the waist down, the great drooping bulge of her belly angling toward existence. Boselmia watched as her mother experienced a contraction: Maisa's eyes rolled back briefly in her head, and she muttered an unintelligible word from the unintelligible language she sometimes spoke. As she said the words, her hands circled her belly, the movement a prodding more than a maternal caress, as if she were urging the unborn child to hurry along. The unborn child thrashed against Maisa's lower abdomen in response.

The contraction over, Maisa's eyes went to Boselmia. She looked her daughter over with a peculiar frankness, as if scrutinizing her soul. Outside, there was a cry unlike the others, terror-tinged. It sent a shiver of fear galloping down Boselmia's spine. Still, her mother held her gaze.

Maisa continued, "Yes, child. Waisporek is dead. He was a fearsome warrior, but he was not the *Dachahelu*. But *I* am the *Fecheholo*, the only living god of our people, the only person capable of bringing the *Dachahelu* back into existence. Therefore, I must survive. And you are the *Fecheholo's* daughter, destined one day to take my place. Therefore, you must survive. But if we are to survive the night, my child, we must make ourselves capable of terrible things."

Boselmia bit her lip until she drew blood. She wanted to scream at her mother, *"You said that father was the Dachahelu! You said that he would kill our enemies and reign over our people for one hundred years! Why should I believe anything you say?"* But she knew that her lack of belief in her mother's words would in no way affect her mother's convictions. Maisa was a zealous, self-assured woman, certain that any missteps or miscalculation she made was ultimately the design of her own divine providence.

The cries outside suddenly changed to the terror-tinged pitch, accompanied by the trumpeting of musketry. Maisa, unmoved by the sounds, ordered Boselmia to bring her the umbilical knife. Boselmia, numb with grief, did as she was told. With the knife, Maisa made a cut in the fat of her palm. Then she smeared the flowing blood on Boselmia's face and hands. "Go to the door," she commanded. "Lay hands on any who enter and say (   )."

Boselmia heard her mother speak the word, but the instant it was spoken, the word evaded her attempts to grasp it, while simultaneously lingering on the periphery of her purview, like a waking dream not yet forgotten but not wholly remembered.

"Go," Maisa said.

Boselmia did.

Outside, chaos reigned. Parts of the village were ablaze, and Massaporans were dying at the hands of Harrish soldiers now in the midst. Boselmia saw a fair-skinned mother of two named Niiwo run through by a Harrish bayonet, and she saw a hulking Massaporan man named Dashwi choking the life out of one Harrish soldier, before another soldier on horseback lopped off his head with a saber. All was horror and confusion.

When at last she wrenched her eyes away from the carnage, she saw that her mother was giving birth. Maisa was squatting unceremoniously over the dirt floor, her hands positioned to catch the child. In between contractions, Maisa chanted her secret language, whispering the child into the world. Boselmia became entranced by her brother's head, a glossy crowning thatch. She was startled from the reverie when her mother spat her name in warning.

"Boselmia."

9

Boselmia turned to the doorway just as a Harrish soldier stumbled in. He had a rapacious look about him, but before he could take action, Boselmia grabbed him by the arm. The instant she touched him, her mother's word materialized on her tongue. The effect was instantaneous: the man, shot through with pain, collapsed in the doorway.

Uncertain whether the man was alive or dead, Boselmia inched away, only to hear her mother say her name once more. A second Harrish soldier, taller than the first, was stepping over his forerunner's body, savagery in his eyes and a bayonet-tipped musket in his hand. Fortunately, the man's murderous intentions were waylaid by the shock of seeing a woman in labor. Before he could recover, Boselmia lurched forward and grabbed him by the leg, the word once again leaping to her tongue.

Soldier number two fell to the floor. Unmistakably dead.

Maisa spoke Boselmia's name for a third time. Boselmia braced for yet another intruder, but, when it was clear that one wasn't coming, she turned to her mother. Disoriented by the violence she had committed, the sight of the strange, green-eyed babe in her mother's arms compounded her bewilderment. Her newborn brother wasn't at all what she had expected. He appeared in full possession of his motor skills, and he had a lordly bearing that was eerie for a child so young. She searched his face for a deeper understanding. When they locked eyes, she felt a flush of strength rush over her. Not only that, she felt liberated from the shackles of consciousness: her body thrummed with an instinctual passion, one that commanded her, at that very moment, to go outside and tear the enemy of her people to shreds.

She heard her mother speaking as if from a distance. The words jarred her from her trance. She tore away from her brother's gaze.

"He commands the others, Boselmia. Not us."

Boselmia nodded. She made certain to keep her eyes on her mother, and not let them drift back into her brother's orbit.

Maisa continued, "I thought that I could turn your father into the *Dachahelu*. But where I failed with Waisporek, I have succeeded with your newborn brother. The *Dachahelu* lives again."

The *Dachahelu*. The Deer King. Though she dared not look at him, Boselmia could sense her brother's deific presence the way one senses an electrical storm; he possessed a current of strength capable of reshaping the world.

"Tonight, he is our only hope to stay alive," Maisa said. "When we make our escape, your brother will try to command you, but you are not his to command. Repeat this word after me: ( )."

She repeated the word back to her mother, although she wasn't sure how she managed the pronunciation. Maisa nodded. "When you feel him try to command you, say the word again and again. Stay close to me when we escape. The *Dachahelu* is small, but he will try to fight the Harrish. We must not let him. If he fights now, he will die. If he struggles to go free and I begin to falter, you must restrain him, at all costs. The others will die protecting us. It is an honor we will not deny them."

She nodded that she understood.

Boselmia watched as Maisa gathered a pair of buckskin breeches and dressed her bruised and bloodied lower half. Together they walked outside. Boselmia noticed her mother's unsteady gait, and only then did the reality of Maisa's condition dawn on her: she had fought in a battle and given birth on the same day.

High above, the peeling moon watched with interest. Boselmia guided her weakened mother and newborn brother away from the bloodletting. She needed to find a horse, any horse. She moved toward the back of the village, where the horses were often tied. But the village chaos encroached, threatening to consume. Seeking a clear route, Boselmia snuck behind a house on the village edge, only to find two Harrish soldiers raping a Massaporan woman. Or no, not a woman, but a child, a friend: Jaan, a slightly older girl whom Boselmia had always secretly idolized, lay dead-eyed beneath a rutting Harrishman, while the other soldier hovered above her head, pinning her arms to the ground.

Her shock at what she was witnessing was quickly supplanted by the force of her newborn brother's will. The flush of strength that she had felt earlier overheated into an all-enveloping energy: her identity was subsumed into the life-force of the Massaporan collective, a spiritual organism driven by the *Dachahelu's* passions. *Kill those men,* her brother commanded. She started to obey, but before she could put instinct to action her mother reached out, touched her by the arm, and reminded her of the word.

Boselmia instinctively repeated it, and the spell was broken.

She turned her attention back to her friend. Jaan was under the spell's thrall: Boselmia watched with wild wonder as her friend's eyes turned to green fire and she struck back against her attackers. Jaan lunged forward and bit her rapist on the nose, then wrenched free from the other soldier and grabbed his unattended sword from off the ground. She slashed the sword at the rapist, cutting his leg. The soldier howled in pain and rolled off her, but before Jaan could inflict further damage, the soldier near her head manacled her arms with his hands.

Hypnotized by the struggle, Boselmia didn't realize what was happening around her. The Massaporan people were gathering at a fevered pitch, eyes alight with green flame, flocking to the *Dachahelu* like proverbial moths. Sensing their presence, Boselmia turned and saw what her brother's magic had wrought: emerald-eyed Massaporans were fighting against the Harrish with a stunning strength, fueled by the *Dachahelu's* presence. But there was also a formlessness to their collective purpose: they were waiting for the *Dachahelu* to lead them. He, however, was his mother's captive: before he could lead, he had to escape her grip. Which he was trying to do. Boselmia watched her brother buck against Maisa with a wild abandon, every movement bringing him closer to freedom.

Boselmia grabbed her newborn brother's legs just as he slipped free from Maisa's grip. With his head still propped against Maisa's bosom, the Deer King twisted his body around and, with an expressionless face, launched himself at Boselmia, attempting to butt her with the crown of his head. She jerked away, his head missing her chin by less than an inch. Gravity's boomerang returned the Deer King to his mother's arms. Maisa grabbed him by the wrists with a renewed strength. Together they overpowered him.

After a moment's resistance, the Deer King stopped fighting, and instead turned to look at his mother and sister with a distant perplexity, the way a general on a hilltop might react to a mutinous regiment on the battlefield below. His eyes were aflame with visions of the past: in the bottomless wellspring of his pupils, Boselmia saw a tall, antlered man standing amidst a field of bronze-skinned corpses, the colossal jawbone of an unidentified animal in one hand and a blood-slicked hatchet in the other. Mesmerized, Boselmia felt her will dissolving once more, until her mother's voice rang high and clear above the din.

"I am the *Fecheholo*, goddess of the Massaporan people, and redeemer of the *Dachahelu*! The *Dachahelu* may hold you with his gaze, but I hold you with my words! Know this: those who fight with the *Dachahelu* tonight hasten his death, but those who sacrifice their lives so that the *Dachahelu* may escape will usher in a future that belongs to all the Massaporan people. So I command you: save your god. Now!"

And then, in a loud and clear voice, she repeated the word she had shared with Boselmia, diluting the *Dachahelu's* spell.

At first the Massaporans hesitated, caught between the commands of competing gods. But then, in a rush, they complied. Like a wave forming from the belly of the Ocean of Sighs, the survivors of the night's atrocities caught up Boselmia and her mother and brother in the surf, and made to deposit them on a safe shore. But their numbers were few, and the Harrish were many. The soldiers, who had been scattered to the winds of the village in their attempts to hunt down the Massaporans, now converged on the *iiwase*-touched survivors, and tried to land the finishing blow.

Boselmia saw flashes of the fight. She was half running, half being carried by a corporeal shield of Massaporans. Through the gaps of flesh she saw a smattering of Harrish soldiers forming a line to her left, their muskets raised. There was a sound like the heavens opening and a gash of hellfire, and the shield of Massaporans thinned, bodies collapsing in the dirt. But still the group pressed on. Glancing around, Boselmia thought she saw Jaan running astride the group. She rejoiced that her friend had fought off her attackers, but then the girl peeled away to fight the pursuing Harrish, and Boselmia's sense of joy vanished. The world was a frenzy of violence and death, and the picture it painted was an ever-evolving portrait of destruction; it was impossible to say who or how many had died, only that many had sacrificed themselves, and many more were prepared to.

At last, they reached the horses. She mounted one, her mother and brother another. At a glance, there appeared to be eight Massaporans remaining in their company, but then four of the villagers broke away to attack a small band of Harrish soldiers who had followed them into the copse of trees where the horses were tied. She followed their green eyes, which were like lanterns in the dark, until the violent clash of bodies snuffed the lanterns out.

In the midst of this sacrifice, they galloped away. Boselmia, Maisa, the *Dachahelu*, and four others. North, toward *Jaironim*. The woods and the dark enclosed them in a maternal embrace. The horses, familiar with the trail, took to the flight with poise and energy, eager to leave the warfare behind.

Only the hooves of death followed. Two minutes down the trail they heard the stark sounds of their pursuers closing in. Without a word, the other riders in their party turned back. Boselmia, an accomplished rider, considered falling back with them: how many would perish to save their lives? But her mother's voice cut through the night like a scythe, "No." She looked at her brother and mother and saw the price of her rebellion: the *Dachahelu* had used the opportunity of Maisa's broken chant to try and break free from the *Fecheholo's* grip. Somehow, Maisa recovered, holding fast to the boy and to the horse's mane while starting up the chant again, until the words, like a balm, brought the *Dachahelu* to heel. Even the darkness couldn't conceal the epic nature of their struggle: the *Dachahelu's* green eyes were cinders illuminating both his strength and Maisa's epic resolve.

The night was a cloak; they wound their way into the safety promised in its fabric, the fleeing gods of a people who had died to protect them. The silence expanded. After a time, it became clear that they were no longer being followed. But on they continued, into deeper and darker woods, the night like a gentle predator swallowing their past lives whole.

When daylight broke, they had reached *Jaironim*.

3

199 A.D.

Boselmia and Notel stopped on the banks of one of the Yippikuri's northernmost tributaries, its blue waters like an inverted sky. The boy had been quiet since they had left the village. This wasn't abnormal, but there was a latent quality to this particular silence that made it more ominous than most. Boselmia knew that Notel (he had been named after the second Deer King) had a gentler nature than his predecessors, but he wasn't above fits of pique. Generally, Boselmia could tell when he was on the verge of one. She sensed one now.

Its eruption was a thing to behold. With a feral recklessness that belied his previously measured state, the boy bounded about the banks of the river with a mad animal energy, all sinew and strength. The emotions that he otherwise struggled to express poured out of him: he jumped and tore the lower branches of trees with his bare hands; he dug at the dirt with his heels; he even head-butted the wind, a sight that should have looked ridiculous, only his ferocity didn't allow it. In one fantastic display, the boy leapt over the water, grabbed hold of a suspended tree branch, and swung his body back to shore in a single, fluid motion. And to think that he was scarcely one year old.

The sight of the *Dachahelu* tapping into the boundless store of his physical power made Boselmia feel inadequate to the task before her. She had never had her mother's gift for molding these creatures into the purposeful war gods they were intended to be. She supposed it was because she was too much like them. How she wished she could switch places with the boy: oh, to be told that one's sole purpose in life was to wreak havoc and destruction. She would have been a master of it. Ha, she *was* a master of it! If only she had the Dachahelu's physical tools to match, she would have ridden Tsadanali of the Harrish scourge decades before.

Or so she liked to believe.

When at last he was spent—or perhaps merely sated—the boy wandered over and sat at Boselmia's feet. He had worked himself into quite a state, as evidenced by the verdant bloodbath filling up his eyes: for the briefest of seconds Boselmia saw her son—the short-lived Riiyisti, the fifth Deer King—laying waste to the motley masses in Selwick. The sight of him jarred her. But then Notel spoke in a calm and direct voice, and Boselmia reclaimed the present.

"Where are we going?"

"North. Away."

"Why?"

"I told you. So that you may live."

He sat with her answer the way one might sit with an unwanted guest. Riiyisti appeared in the *Dachahelu's* eyes again, and, disturbingly, so did the half-breed vagabond who had killed him— the Torquecan. Boselmia watched as the Torquecan's *olorusco*- addled, wraith-like figure stole up behind her offspring's throat, dagger in hand. Boselmia refused to flinch, and, as if answering an unspoken prayer, Riiyisti and his killer vanished.

"I miss the girl," the boy said.

The *Dachahelu* was lovesick over the Stoneman's daughter, the same girl whose father had stood waiting for Notel to exit the birth canal so that he could slit the boy's throat with a dagger. Boselmia recalled the girl's name. Emmaline. Emmaline Rain.

She eyed the boy with contempt. These matters required a certain delicacy that she no longer possessed. *"The girl is Harrish. The girl is your enemy. You were meant to kill the Harrish. Not love them. You were meant to kill her."*

The flames in the boy's eyes exploded, their lapping mouths tasting the whites of his eyes. A formidable, antlered shadow claimed the stage of his pupils: the god at the core of the boy, the *Dachahelu* as he was before *Funato* smote him and brought about the dawn of conscious time.

The boy spoke with a booming timbre. *"I am meant to rid Tsadanali of the plague of people who have muddled the meaning of existence. I am meant to return those who would follow me to my waking dream, and there grant them the freedom to live life the way it was intended to be lived, without word or thought or conscious deed."*

She couldn't give a fuck what Notel or the other gods inside of him thought. *"You're meant to kill the Harrish is what you're meant to do,"* she sneered at him. In all her years she had only seen the original *Dachahelu* three times—this was the fourth. But as far as she was concerned, he was dead and gone, and she would be damned if anyone—yes, even the god whose supremacy she had spent her entire life trying to restore—was going to tell her that the paramount reason for bringing the *Dachahelu* back to life wasn't to extinguish the life of every last Harrish settler.

The apparition disappeared. The boy's *iiwase* contracted to a degree that he was mostly boy and only slightly god, the green of his eyes cooling to a crystalline appearance. When he spoke, his voice was a whisper. *"She sat with me through the night. She held me in her arms."*

Boselmia guffawed. She ignored the pinprick of pain needling her heart, brought on by her own memories of caring for Riiyisti. She reminded herself that she had done her son a disservice in the end: because of her maternal coddling, Riiyisti had died faster than any *Dachahelu* before him, and with less glory. Her mother's words resounded in her skull: *The Harrish do not soften their steel. They sharpen it. The next time you care for a weapon, you'd be wise to treat it as one.*

She oiled her tongue. *"That girl's father was the Stoneman. Do you know who the Stoneman is?"*

The boy didn't reply. Though of course he knew who the Stoneman was. She had lectured him on the subject dozens of times.

She continued, *"The Stoneman is a man whose sole purpose in life is to kill the Dachahelu the instant he is born. When this Stoneman—the girl's father—failed to kill you, the Harrish killed him. That girl has now returned to Haven, where she will be taught that you are the essence of evil, and that the Harrish people can never be safe until you are dead. They will choose another Stoneman, or, better yet, raise an army, to come and kill you. And if the Stoneman or the army is successful, that girl, like every Harrish man and woman, will rejoice."*

Somewhere out over the water a fish took flight, re-entering the river with a graceless *plop*. The *Dachahelu*, who already knew everything Boselmia had just told him, let his gaze drift away. He wasn't being defiant—he, nor any of the *Dachahelus* before him, possessed the subtlety necessary for passive resistance—but, as was customary with his kind, when he was presented with information that he didn't want to hear, he cast his attention elsewhere.

Boselmia experienced a flash of anger. One of the three sacred words that a *Fecheholo* uses to control the *Dachahelu* leapt to her lips, but she managed to restrain herself before speaking the word and forever diluting its power. Using the words too often too early was a mistake she had made with Riiyisti, one she was determined not to repeat.

She settled on a different tact. *"You may not like what I have to say, but that doesn't mean it isn't true."*

Slowly, the boy's eyes resettled on hers, the green flames dancing once more. She had the sensation, as she often did when she was conversing with the boy in the old tongue, that the one-year-old was much older and wiser than she was. She felt his judgment amassing like a storm cloud.

"Your truths are your own, Fecheholo. They do not belong to me."

The word came then of its own accord. Spiraling, as all the old words did, out of the cavernous heart of the Black Riddle. Her bloodstream quickened as the *jwonatuwe* returned to her lips like an illicit lover—and then, because she was a god, because she and her mother had traveled into the Black Riddle where the language of creation was written, she spoke the word into existence, and, in doing so, bound the *Dachahelu* to her will.

The boy, already as still as pond water, became as motionless as a rock. He was hers to control. But behind his burning green eyes, Boselmia thought she detected the boy's defiance. He knew that she had made a mistake. *She* knew that she had made a mistake. It seemed the only thing left to do was to make the most of her error.

She made her voice as hot as roasting coals.

"Pray that you never see the girl again, Notel. For if you do, I will bind my will to yours, and make you ravage the girl until she is utterly destroyed. Your last memory of her will be of her heart as you feast upon it. Then you will carry that memory with you for the remainder of your days."

He didn't react. She wanted to abase him, to make him see the extent of her power over him, but she had brought him under her control for no purpose other than to satisfy her temper, and with each moment that passed, she was left with the choice of either repeating the word again until she could decide upon a proper degradation, or releasing him and admitting her folly.

The seconds ticked by until she had made the decision by default.

Free from Boselmia's control, the boy began to move in a strange way, flooding the blood into his extremities by pushing out rhythmic waves from his core, the whole of him flopping like a beached fish. When he was finished, he stood and stared off into the distance, pretending as if what had just happened had not occurred. Boselmia studied him, and found herself wondering, as she sometimes did, who this boy truly was. Like every *Dachahelu*, he was an amalgam of the Deer Kings who had come before him, but he was also himself, a being like no other. As he was not yet fully formed, it was difficult to tell where the others Deer Kings ended and where he began. But she thought perhaps she had just been afforded a glimpse of the real him. It seemed that he was made of both sterner and softer stuff than his predecessors.

He turned and looked at her. His eyes were his own.

Your truths, he said, repeating himself, *do not belong to me.*

They walked north. The direction of retreat. With every mile, the massive dew oaks grew more massive still, their gnarled trunks like the sunken, decrepit faces of forgotten gods. Occasionally, bitter bursts of wind snapped through the woods, teasing Boselmia's and the *Dachahelu's* flesh in a mean sort of way. As a distraction, Boselmia drew a *bittirinu* from the recesses of her cloak and chomped on the end, savoring the flaky sweetness. Bits of tobacco clotted on her tongue. She wanted a light, but she didn't want to take the time to summon a fire.

While they walked, she thought about how much she hated the north, how much she hated Wolfresh. She had not been raised here: she had been raised in *Toway*, where the settlers lived now, in the northern part of the territory the Harrish called Haven. Wolfresh was a made-up place, an amalgamation of the old Jindois lands *Breswan* and *Jaironim*. Wolfresh was the name given to the place where the Harrish had forced the Massaporans to live, named after the Massaporan who had capitulated to Harrish demands— Wolfresh. *The Great Peacemaker,* they had called him, both the Harrish and, surprisingly, a fair number of Massaporans: there were still those who believed that Wolfresh had saved the Massaporans from extinction by allowing them to be corralled like cattle. But Boselmia, like her mother before her, knew better. The Harrish had been advancing steadily north and west ever since Edward Drey first landed on the eastern shores of Tsadanali. They would resume their bloody expansion soon enough.

Ah, there they are.

Ahead, scattered among the colossal dew oaks and sturdy blood elms, scores of Massaporan corpses lay atop suspended deerskin hides. The hides were stretched and tied to wooden stakes jutting out of the ground. Below the corpses and the deerskin hides, deep pockets of earth waited like patient mouths. It was one of the largest Massaporan burial grounds in all of Wolfresh, located this far north because it was far enough away from Harrish lands that the Massaporans felt comfortable practicing their old ways.

Boselmia looked for a corpse nearing descension. She spotted one near the trunk of a knotty jorkwood tree: half of a skeleton was tangled in the web of a rotting deerskin. The skeleton's lower half had fallen into the pit below, while the upper torso clung to the deerskin, waiting on the moment in the not too distant future when it too would tumble into the abyss.

Notel, who had been trailing behind Boselmia, pulled even. Boselmia glanced at him long enough to see that his marveling eyes were not touched by *iiwase*. She considered explaining the Massaporan burial rituals to the boy in the old tongue. But then, not wanting to spoil the simmering hostility between the two of them, she decided against it. She headed into the maze of corpses and open graves without looking to see if Notel was following her.

It was unbecoming for a Massaporan to leer at the departed, but Boselmia wasn't your typical Massaporan: she was the *Fecheholo*, the Raven Queen, a god. She walked the farrago of pits, glancing inside, recalling now and again whose skulls and spinal columns graced which holes. Inside the pits, the skeletons were a jumble: the Massaporans believed that one's mortal remains desired the same end as their souls—to lose their sense of identity and rejoin the collective. Hence the communal graves. But Boselmia rejected such dogma: she had no intention of relinquishing her identity in the afterlife, and she didn't expect others to, either.

Finally, she found the pit she was most interested in seeing. Boselmia peered inside to where her lover Ayyit's bones now rested. She quickly identified her friend's long and narrow skull. Ayyit's jaw was slightly open and facing skyward; it looked like she was having a laugh at having died, which was exactly the sort of thing Ayyit would have found funny.

"You're mocking me for still being alive, aren't you?" Boselmia asked the skull. "Laugh it up, you old biddy," she continued, not without affection. "When my time comes, I'll make sure they suspend me over this very hole, and when the deerskin rots, I'll come crashing down and wipe the smile off your face."

She felt better after the exchange. It was good to see Ayyit, even if she was dead. They had been lovers once: being the *Fecheholo* made it difficult to form real bonds, but Ayyit's strong, silent behavior had dovetailed nicely with Boselmia's prickly mien, and, as is so often the case, they found ways to find the softness in each other that the rest of the world assumed they lacked.

She sensed the boy standing beside her. He had finally caught up to her. She looked down at him. Checked his eyes. Still *iiwase*-free.

"Do you want to know who she was?" she asked the boy in Massaporan, knowing he wouldn't understand. He neither looked at her nor responded; instead he stared at Ayyit's skull, mesmerized. Capitalizing on his obliviousness, she continued, "Her name was Ayyit. When my mother died breaking the world in two, Ayyit brought me into her home and made me whole again. Then, when I bitched and moaned about the trials and tribulations of being the new *Fecheholo,* she stuck her tongue in my snatch until I forgot what I was bitching and moaning about."

She was silent for a moment. She enjoyed being profane—it had always seemed to her one of the few true joys of life—but this time her vulgarity struck a hollow note in the echo chamber of her soul. Before she knew what she was doing, she let her guard down and spoke the painful truth. "I refused to bring you into the world until after she died. I watched the Stoneman slit a hundred of your brothers' throats so that I could enjoy my last days with her, and I would have gladly watched him slit yours as well had doing so granted me a precious few more hours with Ayyit."

Notel, as expected, didn't respond. Instead, he took a step toward the communal grave and rested on his haunches, staring deep into Ayyit's eyes. The sight of the *Dachahelu* staring at her former lover made Boselmia's temper flicker. *Little piss-ant,* she muttered in the old tongue. She turned and stalked off into the woods before he could react.

She knew exactly where she was heading. As good as it was to see Ayyit, there was someone else she had come to visit: the traitor, Doido Mass. Turning north and west away from the burial ground, she made her way toward the spot where the southernmost wiswake tree in all of Tsadanali stood. She walked close to forty yards before finding it, its slender limbs beckoning like an old friend.

Upon reaching the tree, she gave its silvery-purple bark a hard brush. A dusting of resin stuck to her hand. She waved her palm under the sunlight streaming through the trees. The wiswake pitch shone resplendent, like stardust. *Good medicine,* she thought. For a moment her mind went to her daughter Shayo, and to her daughter's Breekish spouse, Oostri. She said a soft prayer (To who? Herself? She couldn't say) that the wiswake paste she had gifted to Shayo in exchange for the Stoneman's daughter had failed to reach Oostri in time.

"Hopefully my daughter's ugly, turtle-looking husband is as dead as you are by now, Doido," she said out loud, laughing. Still chuckling, she found the V-shaped branch that pointed like a slingshot to the traitor's grave. *Ten steps east, four paces off the dew oak, seven off the blood elm.* She counted off the steps with a buoyant flair, settling over what she knew was the right spot. Then she hiked her deerskin skirt up around her thighs, squatted, and took a long, hot piss.

"Wake up, down there!" she cackled. She fell into a fit of laughter as she recalled the look on Doido's face when she had buried him, his expression frozen in a frigid rictus. The joy it gave her to know that he was still down there now, his skeleton miming the same dumbfounded look, his mortal remains wasting away in isolation instead of in a communal grave—why, it was almost enough to make an old woman feel that her life hadn't been entirely futile.

She finished urinating. Pulled her skirt back down. Then she stepped away from the grave, and sat cross-legged on the ground. She fished her hand inside the raven-feather cloak, rummaging for the stone in one of the pockets. Her fingers located it with a cool caress. She presented it to the pissed-on plot of earth with a flourish.

"Look what I have, Cloudworm! One of your pebbles! Can you imagine that? Me, your mortal enemy, in possession of one of your precious stones! And after you worked so hard to ensure that they would never fall into my hands. But it was all for naught. And I'm not done yet. Oh no. I'll have the second one too before this is over."

Without missing a beat, she cupped her ear to the ground. "What's that? Yes, you sniveling scum. I *have* brought another *Dachahelu* into the world. Come again? Well, of course you're worried that the Harrish will raze our villages and wipe our people off the face of Tsadanali. Because you're a coward. And like any coward, you have no sense of the lengths the brave will go to defend their way of life. It's why you're dead, and I'm not."

She felt pleased with herself. It was good to insult her old enemy again. If only she could visit Doido's secret grave more often, it might keep her in touch with her purpose as the *Fecheholo*.

She looked up. The boy was coming, trotting up the rise with a disconcerted look on his face. Boselmia smiled, glad for the opportunity to introduce him to Doido. She hadn't yet noticed Notel's unease.

"Oh Doido, this is a sweet day indeed! First, I get to piss on your grave, and now I'm going to have the *Dachahelu* trample all over it. If you'll wait here…"

She started to cackle again at her joke, but then Notel's *iiwase*-singed eyes caught her own, and she registered his ruffled manner. She stood up to meet him. The *jwonatuwe* kicked into gear, coursing through her adrenaline-flooded system as it dawned on her that something was wrong. She searched for a word in the old tongue, one to illuminate the peril, but then she saw *it,* saw *them,* weaving through the maze of graves on a trio of horses, heading toward her and the boy.

Doshensa. Etu. Aagili.

Three of the seven *Koeceti.*

4

140 A.D. – 145 A.D.

Boselmia's newborn brother's name was Yestric. He was the fourth *Dachahelu,* or Deer King. Maisa spent her time fashioning him into a weapon that would one day terminate the Harrish scourge, so Boselmia tried as much as was possible to teach him how to be a boy. How to be her brother. Together, the three of them went from village to village, basking in the devotion of the Massaporan people, who worshipped them all but revered Yestric; at every stop they begged him for the favor of a touch, of a look, of an answered prayer. But Maisa held him apart and aloft, above his people. "Beg not of the *Dachahelu,*" she would reproach them. "Instead, prepare yourself to be an instrument of his will." And the people, afraid of Maisa, would cower, and bow, and leave Yestric alone.

It was a difficult time to be a Massaporan. The tribe was still licking its wounds over the catastrophic defeat at the Yipikurri River and the subsequent loss of the *Toway* lands, a defeat for which, Boselmia came to understand, many blamed Maisa. Delivering the *Dachahelu* from the ashes of the battle had been her saving grace. "The *Fecheholo* always shoulders the blame. Remember that. But the *Fecheholo* also shows the way," Maisa told Boselmia. "After the death of Notel, also known as the second *Dachahelu,* the fifteen successive male heirs of the great chieftain Maiso all attempted to resurrect our lord and king, and they all failed. But when the male line died out, the sixteenth heir—Bo, your namesake—traveled first into the Impossible Mountains, and then deep into the Black Riddle, where she learned the language of creation and was able to speak the *Dachahelu* once more into existence. We are the keepers of that line. We are the women who risk everything so that our people may once again live inside the *Dachahelu's* waking dream."

Boselmia wanted to believe her mother. Maisa had, after all, traveled deep into the Black Riddle and there learned the old tongue, the first person since Bo to have done so. It was why Maisa wore the cloak of the *Fecheholo*, why she possessed powers that no mortal should attain. But Boselmia was also a witness to the tears in

24

the fabric of Maisa's godhood: her false prediction that she had transformed Waisporek into the *Dachahelu*, her slippery grasp on power, her shortcomings in rearing Yestric. Boselmia believed her mother the way that most teenagers believe their parents: she was old enough to see the cracks in Maisa's proclamations, even though the child in her desperately wanted to believe that her mother's every word was true.

When Yestric was five years old, they traveled into a village on the western banks of the northern Yipikurri. For months they had heard tales of the growing clout of a chieftain who lived there, a man by the name of Wolfresh. He was known primarily for his diplomatic skills: he had traveled extensively in the west, and was respected by both the Effanarem people and those brave motley souls who made a living trading goods in the harbor lands. As the Massaporan nation no longer had a functioning hierarchy, Wolfresh had become as powerful as any Massaporan alive, with the exception of perhaps the *Fecheholo* herself. Word reached Maisa that Wolfresh hoped that she would soon visit, so that he and his villagers could pay both her and the *Dachahelu* the respect they were due. He also promised to treat her to a feast to end all feasts. Maisa, accustomed to being courted, pledged that her little family would come.

When they arrived, however, the scene was far different than what they had anticipated. The village had been prepped for the festivities—intricate and colorful garlands hung from wooden stakes, and the air was redolent with charred venison and freshly cooked whitefish—but the village was also ghostly quiet, seemingly devoid of souls. They wound their way to the village's heart, seeking the answer to the mystery, until at last they came upon three men sitting around a fire pit: two Massaporans and a strange, shaven-headed man with an elaborate series of earrings cascading down his left earlobe.

"*Fecheholo*," said the least conspicuous of the trio, standing to greet them. "Thank you for the honor of your presence. I am Wolfresh." Wolfresh was a small, brown bear of a man, in the stage of life where his weathered features enhanced rather than detracted from his attractiveness. His smile was warm and sincere, but also knowing; he made no effort to pretend that he hadn't staged their arrival for some specific if yet undetermined purpose.

Maisa refused to meet his eyes. Boselmia, trying to hide her growing worry, mimicked her mother's imperious gaze.

"You have a foreigner with you," Maisa said at last, nodding at the bald man. She was slightly taller than Wolfresh, and she used it to her advantage, moving closer to him so that the discrepancy in their height was obvious.

"I do," stated Wolfresh. "But first, allow me to introduce my nephew." He pointed to the other Massaporan at the fire, a long and curly-haired teenager who looked like a collection of poorly stacked bones, or perhaps a minor god's ill-humored attempt at combining a human with a stork. "His name is Doido." The boy, taking umbrage with the introduction, jutted his chin at Wolfresh. "Doido Mass," Wolfresh clarified. "Like myself, he is a direct descendant of Maiso, the first Massaporan chieftain." It was once common practice among Maiso's descendants to add *Mass* to the end of their name, although the practice had died out somewhat after the coming of the third *Dachahelu*. The boy nodded, content with the clarification.

As with Wolfresh, Maisa refused to look at the boy. Boselmia tried to follow suit, but the boy was too intriguing to ignore completely. She stole a couple of glances at him, curious why he was being afforded a seat at such an important affair.

"And you are?" Maisa demanded of the man with many earrings, before Wolfresh could introduce him.

The man's gourd-yellow eyes wandered the planes of existence until they located Maisa's. "Ash," he replied. It was unclear from the distant look on his face if he was referring to his name or the state of his mortal soul.

"Where is this man from?" Maisa asked, turning on Wolfresh. "And where are the villagers?" Her voice was so fierce that Boselmia shuddered.

Wolfresh folded his hands together and rested them on the knoll of his belly. He let his eyelids grow heavy, and his gaze turn dull. "Ash is from *Biiyegri*. Where the Keebro people live. The villagers are not here because you and the *Dachahelu* have the power to use them as a weapon. And I have something to tell you that you may not enjoy hearing. Something that may compel you to lash out at me."

He said what he said so plainly, so matter-of-factly, that it didn't sound real.

"I don't need the villagers to kill you, old man," Maisa responded.

Wolfresh smiled, a simple grin that bespoke a strange, quiet confidence. "That may be true. Though I hope to not find that out."

He continued to hold his grin, and then he looked around, bestowing his smile first on Boselmia and then on Yestric, whom he studied with an avuncular affection. "Behold," he said, gesturing at Yestric, "a god in the flesh."

Ash nodded dreamily, his eyes half-shut. Doido smirked.

Maisa gave Wolfresh a look of withering contempt. "The *Dachahelu* is not simply *a* god. He is *your* god. You should kneel before your god," she said, challenging Wolfresh with her stare. A scythe-like contour shaped her lips. "Kneel," she commanded.

Wolfresh took a step back, his strange, quiet grin once more in place. He began lowering himself to the ground, and, for a moment, seemed to be falling to his knees. But rather than obey, he merely reclaimed his seat around the fire. "Do you know who the Keebro people are, *Fecheholo*?" he asked once seated.

Maisa's expression was a firestorm of rage. She refused to answer, although whether this was because she was angry or because she didn't know the answer to the question, Boselmia wasn't sure.

"I am not surprised," Wolfresh said, taking her silence for a *No.* "Many do not. Although as a god, it would benefit you to know the history of all the Tsadanali people." He paused, letting the slight sink in. "Your name is Maisa," he continued, seemingly switching subjects. "You are named after Maiso then, the first chieftain of the Massaporan people?"

"I am," Maisa stonily replied. Boselmia knew that Maisa was proud of her namesake. She had given it to herself after emerging from the Black Riddle. Her first name had been lost to time.

Doido, sitting cross-legged on the grass, smirked yet again.

"You know then, of the history of Maiso's brothers?"

"I know of Effanar," she answered. Wolfresh waited patiently for her to expound. Perhaps because Maisa wanted to disprove Wolfresh's suggestion that she knew too little Massaporan history, she did. "When the Jindois people split in two, Effanar remained behind with those who wanted to continue worshipping the Rain God, *Funato*. Those who left with Maiso to worship the *Dachahelu* became the Massaporans. Those who remained behind became the Effanarem. The Effanarem believe that the *Dachahelu* is an abomination," she finished, sneering.

"They believe that the *Fecheholo* is an abomination as well," Wolfresh responded, a roguish glint in his eye. He continued before Maisa could offer a retort. "There was another, younger brother. Kee. Kee agreed with Effanar that Maiso had committed a grave sin by choosing to worship the *Dachahelu*, but, unlike Effanar, he wasn't convinced that the tribe could continue worshipping *Funato* as if the arrival and subsequent death of the second *Dachahelu* hadn't occurred. He became obsessed with the *Fecheholo's* role in the *Dachahelu's* return. And do you know what conclusion he reached?"

As if on cue, Ash began rocking his body gently back and forth in the seated position, while simultaneously bringing a low and distant song to his lips. Doido, the teenager, copied the foreigner, rocking back and forth while singing the same far-off song. The song's eerie melody struck a note of fear in Boselmia's heart.

Wolfresh continued talking as if nothing had changed.

"Kee surmised that the only way the *Fecheholo* could have brought the *Dachahelu* back to life was if she had traveled into the Impossible Mountains and stolen *Funato's* eternal light, which she then used to travel into the Black Riddle and learn the language of creation. But in order to steal the eternal light, Kee believed that the *Fecheholo* must have murdered *Funato*."

Boselmia looked at her mother, who had grown very still at the sound of the foreigner's song. Boselmia knew that her mother wasn't the *Fecheholo* from Wolfresh's story, but she was a Raven Queen. She wondered what mystic secrets Maisa held in her possession, what history she had inherited in order to become a living god.

Ash and Doido's song strengthened, like the current of a river after a rain. Wolfresh pointed a stubby index finger at Maisa. "Kee believed that the *Fecheholo* would one day bring about the end of the world. In his opinion, the *Fecheholo* had killed a god of life to bring back a god of death. He believed that one day the *Fecheholo* would reincarnate a *Dachahelu* so powerful that the gap between our world and *iiwase* would be forever breached, and all living souls visible to the spirit world would perish. He believed that the only ones who would survive were those who remained unseen."

The foreigner's song built until it drowned out the last of Wolfresh's words. Ash and Doido looked lost in the melody's wave, their very corporeality slipping into the undertow. Fear biting at her heart, Boselmia looked to her mother for guidance. Silent words were falling from Maisa's lips—she was summoning the *jwonatuwe*. To Boselmia's right, Yestric's eyes ignited in green flame. Boselmia, powerless, concentrated on her brother, hoping to fall under his spell. If they were on the verge of being attacked, she wanted to fight like a true Massaporan, lost in *iiwase* and tethered to the *Dachahelu's* waking dream.

To her immense relief, she felt the sudden, insistent pull of her brother's will. She succumbed, and, in an instant, the world changed. The evening sun transformed into an ambient, otherworldly gloaming. But Boselmia couldn't process this, not really—her mind had melded to Yestric's, but not only Yestric's: when she turned to look at her brother, she saw not only him but his predecessors as well: Ahuszill, the third *Dachahelu*, stolid and broad-shouldered, the jawbone of a mule in his right hand and a blood-slicked hatchet in his left; Notel, the second of his kind, long and lanky, his gaze serene, a coil of dark, black hair running the length of his spine; and the first *Dachahelu*, nameless, the god at the center of it all, dead since before the dawn of conscious time, his form indistinct, but possessive of a powerful, palpable energy. The *Dachahelus'* bodies were made of flame—green, flickering spirits. Some distant part of Boselmia's mind wanted to linger on the *Dachahelus*, but it was overrun by a stronger urge to destroy the threat.

She turned to face the enemy. They were no longer Ash and Doido, but instead two bursts of green flame, the same as her, only pulsating within the green flame was an ever expanding and retreating reddish-black mass, like a mutating lump of coal. On the periphery of her consciousness she noted her mother, a wild, bright-green conflagration, and also Wolfresh, whose cool, nearly motionless spirit-fire appeared the epitome of calm in the face of the agitated flares surrounding him.

Along with the *Dachahelu*, Boselmia flung herself at the dark-hearted flames, eager to snuff out their souls. But before she could reach them, the two spirits disappeared into the ether. Confusion reigned. For a brief moment the *Dachahelu's* all-consuming will snagged on its own emptiness. As if by instinct, Boselmia turned to the *Fecheholo's* towering firestorm for guidance, but, to her horror, she saw that it was no longer there: the once-mountainous flame had been reduced to a smoldering ruin.

The *Dachahelu* lashed out, warring with the empty air. But there was no one to fight. Boselmia too flailed about, uncertain what action to take. Her soul felt severed from its purpose. An existential dread filled her being, until it seemed that she might die if she remained tethered to the *Dachahelu*. But then Wolfresh's serene spirit moved into the center of the chaos, and, with a deftness that belied its near-motionless form, plucked one of the dark-hearted flames from the ether. Before either the *Dachahelu* or Boselmia or the smoldering ruin of Maisa's flame could react, Wolfresh produced a long knife, and slit open the spirit's throat.

Boselmia crashed back into the present, her link to the *Dachahelu* severed. The blinding sun, unconcerned with discretion, revealed all. Wolfresh was standing over Ash's ear-ringed corpse, the long knife in his right hand. Maisa had fallen to the ground: she appeared stunned and out of sorts. Yestric's eyes were no longer afire with *iiwase*, and he, too, appeared dazed.

Doido Mass was nowhere to be seen.

Boselmia watched in confusion as Wolfresh leaned down and cleaned the blade on the ground, leaving a smear of red on the grass. His movements were calm and methodical. Every few seconds he would glance at Maisa, who was slowly recovering from whatever had befallen her. When she at last appeared fully in possession of her faculties, he addressed her.

"I suppose you have questions."

The feast was quite the affair. Under cover of a pale moon, they ate charred venison, and rabbit hearts, and whitefish; also squash, and link beans, and hot peppers. There was grain alcohol, and merriment, and, as dinner turned into dancing, an expanding drunkenness that subsumed every breathing soul.

Boselmia guarded her brother throughout. Now that the villagers were here, they approached the *Dachahelu* in droves, eager for a closer look. Maisa, usually overprotective, had abandoned Yestric and Boselmia to the wolves. Now and again Boselmia would catch a glimpse of her mother in the midst of the madness, a flask of grain alcohol in hand, circling Wolfresh as Wolfresh circled her, the two of them looking as like to kill each other as they were to fall upon each other in a drunken lust.

As Boselmia sat there, tending her brother, the words Wolfresh had spoken to Maisa kept rattling around in her brain. *"I will fight for the Dachahelu. Those who follow me will fight for the Dachahelu. I was born a Massaporan and I will gladly die trying to bring our people once more into the Dachahelu's waking dream. But know this, Fecheholo. Should the Dachahelu fail, I will move heaven to bring about a lasting peace with the Harrish in the hopes of preserving what's left of our tribe. And I will use every tool at my disposal to stop you from bringing yet another Dachahelu into this world."*

Boselmia stared out at the farrago of Massaporans now dancing under the blue-black sky. She kept trying to spot the ghost in the midst. Doido Mass. The teenage boy who had traveled with his uncle to *Biiyegri* (Greyknot) and there learned from the Keebro how to disappear. The teenage boy who, like Wolfresh, was a direct descendant of Maiso and believed that the *Fecheholo* was an insult to the lineage of male chieftains who had once ruled the Massaporan people. He was still out there, even now, as insurance against Maisa using the *jwonatuwe,* ready to attack if need be.

The rest of Wolfresh's spiel played out in Boselmia's mind. *"After today, the Keebro will never trust me again. They had hoped that I would put the Fecheholo and the newborn Dachahelu in the ground. Now they'll likely send someone to try and assassinate me. But I've learned every trick they would try and use against me. Your family, however, is in danger. Which is why you must stay with me. Know that I am a true Massaporan, and I will protect you from those who would do you harm. Together, we will unite the Massaporan tribe, and prepare our people for the day the Dachahelu leads them into battle. Then, afterward, win or lose, we will make a permanent peace."*

The dark night crested. The villagers, their thirsts and curiosities slaked, began peeling away to spend the night in wooden houses scrambling up the hill away from the banks above the Yipikurri River. Maisa and Wolfresh, it seemed, had disappeared.

Boselmia tried her best to keep her eyes trained on Yestric, and opened for Doido. But as the hours passed, her heavy eyes drifted toward the heavens, where she could see her little brother reflected in the firmament. The *Dachahelu* constellation, a vast tower of stars, rose out of the northern horizon and ascended into the celestial void, the many antler prongs gutting the sky. Her thoughts meandered into the waking void. She imagined escorting Yestric up into the heavens to live among the stars, where he would forever be safe.

She was on the verge of drifting off to sleep when the ghost appeared. Doido stepped out of the darkness the way one steps through a door, an ash-gray cloud dissipating in his wake. Caught off-guard, Boselmia was left with little choice but to accept his presence. She looked to Yestric, expecting green-fire eyes, but he was asleep and, to her surprise, seemingly unaware of the danger.

"Don't worry," said Doido, sitting his rail-thin frame down beside Boselmia. "I won't hurt him."

Boselmia held her tongue, although she cursed her mother in her mind. It was insulting to be left this vulnerable, especially after a day spent skirting death.

Doido sized her up. His look was one of unmistakable condescension. "Do you want to become the *Fecheholo* one day?" he asked at last, the question sounding like an accusation.

Boselmia was taken aback. *Want* had never factored into the equation. She was the *Fecheholo's* daughter; thus, one day, she would become the *Fecheholo*.

"I want to help our people re-enter the *Dachahelu's* waking dream," she replied, trying to put some bite in her words.

Doido laughed. He was certainly cocksure for being nearly the same age as her. She imagined having the ability to disappear into thin air helped with that.

He wasn't finished testing her. "Your mother is a great evil. Did you know that?"

"You plot murdering the god of your people with foreigners and you mean to lecture me about evil?" she retorted, snap-quick. She had spent years cultivating a barbed tongue in her mind; it felt good to at last put it to use.

Doido assumed a serious, no-nonsense mien. "The world was in harmony before the *Fecheholo* upset the balance. We were once

32

the Jindois people, all of us, and we lived in a Tsadanali without Torquecans or Harrish or Breeks. Back then we paid heed to wise men who showed us the right way to live. Now we follow stupid women into stupid wars against enemies that we have no hope of defeating."

He said what he said with a dull sort of meanness, papering over large swathes of history with no context. Boselmia hated him for his ugly certainty, his ignorant self-righteousness. Her next words left her mouth before she had thought them through.

"Why don't you kill us, then? Right here and now. Prove what a big man you are."

His eyes flashed with rage, but then they cooled into something even scarier, a reflective pool of serious consideration. She thought she had never seen anything more frightening: a young man convinced of his own rightness, and willing to kill for the cause. But then the quick sweep of his eyelashes brushed away his thoughts. "I would love nothing more, but my uncle is of a different mind. He thinks the *Dachahelu* can be managed. He thinks your mother can be managed. He sees the kingdoms to our east and the kingdoms to our west and he means to build his own. I think you so-called gods are more trouble than you're worth, but he…"

Before Boselmia knew what she was doing, she had leapt to her feet and pushed the gangly young man to the ground. She hovered over him with balled fists. "Who are you to disrespect the gods of your people? The Massaporan people are nothing without the *Dachahelu*. Nothing without the *Fecheholo*. You would make us slaves."

Her anger had been so pure that she half-expected Doido to cower and relent, but when her rage had passed, she saw that he had summoned an ire to match her own. He grabbed her by the legs and rolled her to the ground, reversing their positions. Pinning her shoulders to the earth, he spat at her. "My mother and father died in *Toway* five years ago because they placed their faith in your mother's magic. They died believing a *Dachahelu* would save them. But I don't live in their world. I've stepped into the gray lands where the powers of minor gods mean nothing. From there, it's easy to see the affairs of mortals clearly. The ways of the Harrish are the future." He paused, weighing his next words. "But there is a place in the coming world for those who don't cling to dying dreams." He glanced over at Yestric, lying asleep on the grass. "Or to dead and dying gods."

His anger diminished so that their mutual antipathy was once again balanced. Boselmia stopped trying to wriggle out of his wiry grip and instead poured hate into her stare, which Doido equaled, the both of them gazing into an infinite abyss. They might have stayed that way forever, but the shuffle and snort of a waking deity drew their attention. They both looked over at Yestric at the same time. He had risen to his feet and was staring at them the way little children sometimes stare at older people, with an unabashed curiosity. Boselmia thought that at any second his eyes would alight with green fire, but the seconds began to pile up, and the fire failed to appear.

"What does he want?" Doido asked Boselmia, easing the pressure off her shoulders. He sounded unnerved.

She truly had no idea. She couldn't comprehend why Yestric hadn't already drifted off into *iiwase* to summon his earlier incarnations. Earlier today he had known that Doido was the enemy. Why didn't he know that now?

The boy drifted closer. The antler nubs on his head jutted into the surrounding darkness, a black-on-black silhouette: it was unclear where the boy ended and the night began. He moved until he was standing directly beside Doido. Boselmia, who still hadn't answered Doido's question, hadn't the foggiest what Yestric was about to do.

The *Dachahelu* reached out and placed his hand on Doido's shoulder. The instant he touched Doido's skin, the green fire in his pupils lit like a struck match.

Yestric spoke out loud, not in the old tongue, but in the Massaporan that Boselmia had been teaching him the past few years.

"My sister bury you one day."

5

199 A.D.

"Three men! All to run down an old woman and a small little boy! And three *Koeceti*, no less! I suppose that if you've summoned the balls to come and catch me, then you must be pissing your breeches worried what the Harrish might do."

"Hello, *Fecheholo*."

It was Doshensa who spoke. *Of course*, thought Boselmia. He had always had his father's fearlessness. Perhaps before the day was over she would reward his courage by pissing on his grave as well.

"Ah, little Stuck-Shit. I know you're a grown man now, Doshensa, and a *Koeceti* at that, but to me you'll always be little Stuck-Shit, the constipated boy wandering around the village with half a turd sticking out of his asshole, crying for help. You should go home, send another *Koeceti* to take your place. I can't take you seriously."

Doshensa didn't bat an eye. He was a calmer man than Doido, harder to fluster. Not that it bothered Boselmia. The joy was in making the effort.

"Where are you taking the boy, *Fecheholo*?"

"The boy?" She changed her tone, channeling pure malice.

"The *Dachahelu*," Doshensa replied, acceding to her wishes. "Where are you taking him?"

"Don't ask me rhetorical questions, Stuck-Shit. You know damn well I'm taking him wherever the hell I please. The real question is: do you and your friends intend to try and stop me? And, on the small chance that you are successful, are you really such a piece of chicken-shit that you would turn the *Dachahelu* over to our enemies?"

Doshensa sighed. It was a sad sigh, the sigh of a man who had spent his entire life trying to preserve his father's legacy, only to have the *Fecheholo*, his father's enemy, rise from the ashes time and again, seeking to unravel it. "The Wolfresh-Potter Accord made it illegal for any Massaporan to worship either the *Fecheholo* or the *Dachahelu*. The *Koeceti* are charged with enforcing this law. Should the *Fecheholo* or an unlawfully born *Dachahelu* come to the attention of the *Koeceti*, the *Koeceti* are charged with assisting the Harrish in bringing the lives of these fallen gods to an immediate end."

Boselmia laughed. A great, roaring caw, the raven's toneless mirth. "Come now, Doshensa. How many in your own village still carve the symbol of the *Dachahelu* into their log homes, or fashion the *Dachahelu's* symbol and hang it from the trees? You've known what I was doing for years, and did nothing to stop it. You and the other *Koeceti* turned your heads, and prayed that the Stoneman would find his mark."

"And now you've killed the Stoneman."

Boselmia wagged a finger at Doshensa. "Why would you say something like that? The Stoneman died in Mossbane. In Haven. Far from here. Far from me. And I doubt he told anyone that the newborn *Dachahelu* remained alive before he passed." She paused, trying to gauge the *Koeceti's* resolve. She thought she detected weakness. "Go home. Let the Harrish come. They'll kill, and rape, and plunder, yes, but they won't find the *Dachahelu*, and they won't find the Funatan Stone. Our people will weather this storm, Doshensa. Whether or not the Accord has been broken is in the eye of the observer, and you know as well as I do that the Harrish have too many pressing problems to stay for long. Then, when the storm is passed, and the boy is older..." she glanced down at the *Dachahelu*, "...we will have our revenge."

Doshensa appeared to consider her proposal. Etu and Aagili, the two lesser *Koeceti*, wore guardedly optimistic expressions, hopeful for the possibility of a last-minute reprieve from battling the feared *Fecheholo*. The forest, which had been unnaturally quiet for the space of the conversation, breathed with life in the form of songbird melodies and the skittering of squirrel paws on bark. But then Doshensa's face hardened, and the deathly quiet returned.

"Prala, your scoundrel brother and my great-uncle Wolfresh's bastard seed, was there when the priest died. And now, on top of the Funatan stone you took from the girl, the second stone is missing as well. Your handiwork is all over this, *Fecheholo*. And when the Harrish come searching for answers, I intent to hand them both of the stones, along with your desecrated scalp."

Boselmia grinned a rotten grin. "You stupid man."

The three *Koeceti* began rocking their bodies and chanting the Keebro's distant, peculiar song. Boselmia ignored them. She reached her hand out to Notel. To her great relief he came to her, so there was no need to waste precious energy binding him to her will. His eyes were alight with green fire, but he was hovering—as he alone of the *Dachahelus* seemed capable—on the border lands of *iiwase*, in league with the spirits but also with an eye on the world he had left behind. Perhaps he understood that there was no one for him to fight.

No one but shadows.

She reached down and placed the palm of her free hand on the ground. She felt the *jwonatuwe* stirring within her, but she didn't rush, instead allowing the elixir of her Black-Riddle-touched soul to charge the deep, dark magic until it seemed it would pour out of her. Only then did she make a request of Tsadanali in the old tongue, a request that she and her mother had suffered greatly to learn how to ask.

Show me the seen and the unseen.

Tsadanali complied. The doors of perception opened wide, and the world, both the seen and the unseen, made itself known. *Iiwase*, the spirit realm, was visible in all its twilight glory, its gauzy haze juxtaposed with five bright green spirits manifested in flame: the half-realized Riiyisti, Boselmia's only offspring; mighty Yestric, dead now these many years; Ahuszill, the *Dachahelu* who ruled; leonine Notel, the first of his name; and the god at the center of it all, the nameless *Dachahelu* from the time before time. They stood beside the boy, the second Notel, ready for battle, ready to destroy those who would harm the Massaporan people. Only they couldn't see the shadows creeping in at the seams, gray people-dreams moving with their knives out, swimming in and out of a fog-like realm.

But Boselmia saw them. It was difficult to parse the multiple realities, but she knew that she must, and so she did, keeping her eyes trained on the *Koeceti*. They moved closer, wary, knowing that she could see them in fits and bursts. As they drew closer they spread apart, hoping to come at her from different angles, but she committed to one, Etu, and with a quickness that belied her old age she jerked the *Dachahelu* with one arm and laid hands on Etu with the other, a terrible word on her lips. She knew the very language that had spoken the world into existence, both the language of creation and the language of destruction. Using this language, she cleaved Etu's body in half with one word.

She paid a price for the victory. Aagili lunged at her from behind, trying to seize on her distraction. Red-hot pain radiated up the *Fecheholo's* side, a slash from a knife. In the process Aagili fell, transforming into an ashy apparition at her feet. She knew better than to fight the momentum of her pain, so she went with it, falling to the ground while simultaneously releasing the *Dachahelu*: in order to save him, she had to let him go. She sensed Aagili scrambling, desperate and eager to capitalize on the opening, but before he could, she redirected the *jwonatuwe* toward her feet, near the spot where she had fallen, and spoke the command of fire. It worked imperfectly: a fireball erupted on the spot, engulfing Aagili in flame, but at the same time it snared the hem of Boselmia's raven-feathered cloak. She rolled away, trying to smother the flame. She put the fire out but not before she had been burned. How badly, it was difficult to say.

She had lost. The reality dawned on her like a cold winter's morning. She had made too many mistakes, and Doshensa remained. Summoning the fire had severed her tether to the multiple layers of reality, and she didn't have the time or the strength to ask Tsadanali to show her the seen and the unseen once more. She looked up into the cavernous blue-white sky and waited for Doshensa. Waited for death.

Only, before death could find her, the *Dachahelu* intervened. Notel rocketed out of the wings and blindly hurled his body at the empty space above Boselmia's prostrate body, slamming into the nothingness there with the nubby crown of his head.

The aftermath was inconclusive. The *Dachahelu*, wild-eyed, didn't know where to direct further attacks, as Doshensa remained concealed by the fog of the gray realms. But Boselmia understood the laws of physics well enough—she gathered her wits and lunged toward the spot where Doshensa had fallen, her hand finding purchase on his body. A dark and unsubtle word leapt to her lips. When she uttered the word, she thought she felt Doshensa's spirit leaving his body. But his corporeal form never materialized, and when she lifted her hand away, she was unable to find him again.

Boselmia collapsed on the grass. It was over. She was badly wounded, yes, but she had the power to heal herself, or at least ameliorate the wounds, if only she could rest a while first. She possessed an inexhaustible supply of *jwonatuwe* inside her very person, but the magic, while a part of her, existed separate from her as well, and it did not act of its own accord without her instruction. For the moment she was broken. Depleted. Old.

She closed her eyes. The agony of her physical condition swept over like a vengeful sandstorm. But as bad as it was, she had weathered worse. She held the pain close, and inside of the pain she imagined the spirits of the *Koeceti* drifting into *iiwase*. Like all mere mortals, they could not control the extent of their spirits' wanderings, and so they drifted on and on, beyond the boundaries of this world.

She laughed.

She opened her eyes. Sunlight bled into her pupils. For a moment, the world was incomprehensible, a tangle of blurs. But soon the central shape blotting her vision formed into a small boy. Notel. The *Dachahelu* who had saved her life. Standing before her.

Something akin to love filled her heart. She felt the temptation of affection. Moved, she tried to remember in her scarred, world-weary heart how best to show the boy that she loved him.

But before she could process her emotions, the *Dachahelu* reared back, and, without warning, slammed the nubby crown of his head hard into her face.

6

145-158 A.D.

The years fell like the trees of the forest: some swift and silent, like the supple jorkwood, others long and slow, like the massive dew oak. The first few years were the dew oaks. They were Wolfresh's captives during this time, even if her mother never admitted it outright. It was a strange captivity: Maisa gave birth to Wolfresh's child—a boy named Prala—and to some degree seemed to make her peace with the captivity. Boselmia kept waiting for her mother to signal their rebellion, their escape, but the signal never came.

In the meantime, Doido lurked, becoming, if not Boselmia's tormentor, than her chief antagonist. Held in check by Wolfresh from fulfilling the worst of his designs (and kept away from Maisa altogether) Doido waited for opportunities to catch Boselmia alone and spew his propaganda, going on and on about the inherent evilness of the *Fecheholo* and the importance of returning to patriarchal rule as it had been during the time of the Jindois. "My uncle agrees with me, you know," Doido would summate in an offhand way, trying to make his vision of the future seem inevitable. "When the *Dachahelu* fails, Wolfresh will kill both you and your mother. But even *if* the little demon succeeds, the *Fecheholo* will never rule by his side. Her days, and yours, are numbered."

Occasionally, Boselmia would find her tongue and wag back. "Your words are empty wishes, Keebro-lover. After my little brother destroys our enemies, your uncle will have no more need of you. He'll send you away to the land of *Biiyegri* that you claim to love so much, with an invading army hot on your heels. Then, when we pluck you up, my mother will have your heart." But despite their mutual threats, the truth was that both of them were uncertain of the adults' designs. Were Wolfresh and Maisa allies now? Or was theirs simply a marriage of convenience, destined to fall apart when Yestric came of age? Boselmia and Doido waited in the wings, uncertain.

In the meantime, Yestric grew. Every year he looked more and more like the god he was meant to be. He was strong, and strapping, and when he crossed over to *iiwase*, he could accomplish feats of daring and strength that boggled the mind. In the latter years—the swift years—Massaporans from all corners of *Jaironim* and *Breswan* came to commune with their god, the one who would lead them to victory and help them retake the *Toway* lands. Afterward, the visitors would stay and talk with Wolfresh and Maisa, plotting the coming war.

One such group was led by a Massaporan chieftain from the far north by the name of Cayap. He came with his wife, Jueshwella, and a particularly fanatical group of villagers, who, it seemed, were especially taken with the *Fecheholo*. Worship of the *Fecheholo* had been muted since Maisa had joined with Wolfresh, but these villagers eschewed the trend, reveling not only in Yestric's presence, but also that of the Raven Queen.

Boselmia was nearly thirty years old by this point. Her young adulthood had been spent in a holding pattern, waiting, like the world around her, for Yestric to grown up. She had yet to take a husband. In all her years she had known only three lovers, all of them one-night affairs that slipped away like passing dreams in the morning light. She knew that she did not like men, but she had convinced herself that her relative asexuality was a byproduct of her and her mother's captivity. She told herself that she had given her mind and body over to a rebellion against Wolfresh, and, to a lesser extent, Doido.

It was around this time that Jueshwella, Cayap's wife, expressed an interest in her. The mother of two small children, Jueshwella at first struck Boselmia as prim and fastidious. Boselmia, who had learned to keep her own company over the years, ignored Jueshwella as she ignored everyone. But one evening, when the others were practicing entering the *Dachahelu's* waking dream, Jueshwella surprised Boselmia by tailing her to an outcrop of rock in the woods where Boselmia often snuck to keep her own council.

"Did you come here to pray for your brother's victory?"

Boselmia, who had been sitting on the highest outcrop, opened her eyes. She was dazed by Jueshwella's presence. Jueshwella had a fawn-like face and eyes the color of a soft, spring sky. She wore her dark brown hair in a plaited braid that hung over her left shoulder like prize game.

"To whom would I pray?" Boselmia responded.

She had meant it as a serious theological question, but Jueshwella laughed it away. Away from the village, away from her husband and children, Jueshwella's entire being opened up, like a flower in bloom.

"It's okay if you're not praying. But you should. I pray to your brother from time to time, and to the first *Dachahelu*, and to Ahuszill as well. Though of course they're all one and the same."

"Do you pray to my mother?"

That laugh again. Boselmia had heard bells once when she was a child, in the last days of trading between the Harrish and the Massaporans. A Harrish trader had tied a string of bright silver bells to his horse's saddle, to draw attention when he entered a village. Jueshwella's laugh sounded like those bells.

"Sometimes," Jueshwella replied, coyly lowering her eyes. Then, more assertively, "My husband does. He tells me late at night that there is more than one battle being fought here. He says that Wolfresh wishes to rule over us all. But Cayap sides with your mother. The *Fecheholo*. He says that we should do whatever is necessary to make sure that regardless of the outcome of our war with the Harrish, the *Fecheholo* leads our people when the war is over."

Boselmia was taken aback. Since the beginning of their captivity, Maisa had scarcely spoken to her of any matter of importance. There were times when Boselmia thought that her mother was fully in Wolfresh's thrall. Her little brother, Prala, was walking evidence of that. So how did Jueshwella and Cayap know of the secret power struggle taking place?

"Are you sure that my mother believes what you believe?"

"Yes."

"And you know this how?"

"My husband's father was one of the first to back Maisa when she emerged from the Black Riddle and proclaimed herself the *Fecheholo*. She has taken Cayap into her confidence, just as she once took his father into her confidence."

"She tells me nothing."

Jueshwella considered this. Her answer was bluntly phrased but softly spoken. "You don't trust your mother. You haven't trusted her since she brought you here. She knows that you don't trust her. That's why she tells you nothing.

Boselmia didn't know what to say. It was true. She didn't trust her mother. But that didn't mean it didn't hurt for her mother not to trust her in turn.

Jueshwella climbed up on the rocks and took a seat beside Boselmia. Without invitation, she ran a finger through Boselmia's hair. Boselmia flinched at her touch. But Jueshwella persisted, continuing to run the same finger through the same strand of hair.

"You enjoy women, don't you?" Jueshwella asked her.

She nodded ever so slightly.

Jueshwella continued, "You are the *Fecheholo's* daughter. One day you will be the *Fecheholo*. You carry a heavy weight. Let me ease your burden."

Boselmia nodded again. She was scarcely breathing. She sensed that all was not as it seemed, but her body ached for Jueshwella's touch, and she found she didn't have the willpower to resist. Jueshwella's finger slipped to Boselmia's shoulder, tracing her shoulder blade around its jutting arc. She might have been drawing a picture of Boselmia's desires, and, in doing so, bringing them to life.

Jueshwella suddenly stopped. Boselmia felt the loss of her touch like a little death. Boselmia thought that if Jueshwella didn't touch her again soon, she might lose her mind.

"Why did you stop?" she asked, nearly begging.

Jueshwella stood up. She hovered over Boselmia like a being from another world. "Come to the place where I sleep tonight."

"But your husband…"

"Come," Jueshwella commanded her. "Your mother needs something from you. And you need something from me. We must both do our parts to bring about the world that we seek."

When Boselmia was older, and she reflected upon her love affair with Jueshwella, it seemed to her that it was a temporary madness beyond her control: her newly awakened cravings and desires overwhelmed her ability to see the truth of the situation, to recognize that she was being used.

On her third night with Jueshwella, Cayap entered the log home and made his way to where Jueshwella and Boselmia were lying. Boselmia stiffened at his presence, but Jueshwella calmed her, and, with a soft but insistent touch, commanded Boselmia to make her peace with it. It struck Boselmia then that Cayap had been with them from the beginning, his inexplicable absence purposeful rather than mysterious. Later, when Cayap lay atop Boselmia and did what he came to do, Boselmia cried soft tears that Jueshwella kissed away with patient lips, each kiss a promise that Jueshwella was hers so long as Boselmia continued to submit.

Cayap came every night thereafter. Boselmia pretended that his intrusions were non-events, a secondary act to the story of her and Jueshwella's love, suppressing the truth in the deepest, darkest corners of her mind: that it was she who was the third party here, a pawn in a game being played by her mother. But it didn't matter. The alternative—refusing the physical affection Jueshwella offered her—was unthinkable. She was determined to believe the fiction until her world came crashing down.

Within months, Boselmia was pregnant. Soon after, the Massaporan people set off for war. The *Fecheholo* ordered the newly pregnant Boselmia north with Jueshwella while nearly everyone else headed south and east. It was a dream of Boselmia's wildest imaginings: every person who had restricted her life—Maisa, Wolfresh, Yestric, Doido, and Cayap—all marched away, leaving her gloriously alone with the love of her life. Together, the two of them headed north for safety, toward Jueshwella's village at the base of the Impossible Mountains.

Only, once they reached there, Jueshwella wanted nothing to do with her. Jueshwella spent her days pining after Cayap, the man whose baby was now growing inside Boselmia's womb. Late one evening, after Boselmia pleaded with Jueshwella to put away her worries for Cayap and come and join her inside the house, something in Jueshwella broke, and she leveled Boselmia with the awful truth.

"Your mother commanded that I seduce you. Otherwise, I would have had nothing to do with you. You're ugly, and you're stupid, and worse, you're a girl. Now my husband's child is in your belly, and he's left me to die at the hands of the Harrish. So leave me alone."

It felt like a mortal wound. Later that night, Boselmia went walking along the shore of a lake that looked like the poured night sky. She weighed her pockets down with rocks and tied them to the inside of her buckskin dress. Then she walked into the shallows of the lake, the cold water speaking its unrepentant language to her skin, a language that said *yes* and *death* and *never again*. She thought that if she communed with the water fully, it might answer all of life's questions in the moments before her death. But when the water reached her gently pooching belly, Boselmia heard a hundred-hooved chorus sounding from the village, accompanied by a tremendous war cry.

She decided that death could wait.

When she reached the teeming village, she learned that Yestric had led the Massaporan people to a tremendous victory. Harrish settlers in the *Toway* lands had been slaughtered by the thousands, and, for the moment at least, the land belonged to the Massaporans once more. Boselmia waded through the masses, looking for a familiar face. These were Cayap's people, returning home. As the many night-cloaked visages passed her by, it dawned on her that the key players—Yestric, Wolfresh, Doido, and Maisa—were likely still south, planning another attack or settling in to defend their gains.

But then her mother materialized from out of nowhere, looking pale and grim and not at all triumphant. Seeing Boselmia, Maisa smiled a sad and heavy smile, an act so out of character that Boselmia understood that something had gone terribly wrong.

"My daughter," Maisa said, raising her hand and stroking Boselmia's cheek, before lowering her hand to Boselmia's belly. Boselmia was too stunned to respond.

Composing herself, Maisa continued. "The *Dachahelu* may win this war, but, even if he does, he will not save us. If he loses, Wolfresh and Doido will come after us with a vengeance. We must leave now, and prepare for what comes next."

They fled into the night. They traveled west, the looming shadows of the Impossible Mountains peering over their shoulders like intrusive giants.

"Where are we going?" Boselmia asked her mother.

Maisa's reply: "The only place left."

By morning light, Boselmia had grown weary, but Maisa continued on with indefatigable verve, a woman possessed. When Boselmia complained that she needed to slow down, Maisa pressed on without responding, seemingly oblivious to Boselmia's condition. Boselmia felt her anger reaching a boil. For years her mother had refused to confide in her or take her needs into consideration. Now, even though Boselmia was pregnant by a man foisted on her by her mother's machinations, Maisa remained indifferent to her suffering.

At midday, Boselmia snapped. She caught up to her mother in a paltry copse of evergreens at the foot of the mountains, jerking her by the arm to grab her attention. "Listen, you bitch," she shouted, the words coming off her tongue like hot flares, "I'll move no more. Not for you."

Maisa laughed, as if Boselmia had said something funny. She had a far-off, distracted look, her eyes scanning the horizon behind them for something, someone. "As you wish. I've already lost Yestric."

Boselmia's curiosity was too strong to resist. "What happened?" she asked.

"In the heat of the battle, he decided that he no longer needed me. Too many bindings over the years—he had learned to exert his own will. I asked everything of him, and it was too much. Whereas Wolfresh asked only that he live in fear of Doido's shadow. And even gods can come to fear death."

Boselmia capitalized on the opening. "You failed. As a mother, and as a god." She relished the sting of the cut as the words left her lips.

Maisa's response was quiet but firm. "Life is full of failure. But still, we persist."

Boselmia made the decision to say what she really wanted to say. "You sow failure and reap destruction everywhere you go. Thousands of our people dead at the Yipikurri River. My father, Waisporek, the supposed *Dachahelu,* among them. Then you create a *Dachahelu* only to lose him to traitors who want us dead." Emotion caught in her throat as she broached the heart of the matter. "And me. You've destroyed me. I thought Jueshwella loved me. But she was only following your bidding."

Maisa's eyes latched onto Boselmia's. "No. You knew she didn't love you. But you were tired of drifting through life. Never taking chances. You are my daughter, but you would rather remain angry at me for not being perfect rather than make mistakes of your own. So you can either blame your life on me—" she pointed at Boselmia's belly, "—or you can claim the child in your belly, and make him a stronger *Dachahelu* than I did Yestric. The choice is yours."

And with those words, Maisa set off again.

Boselmia hesitated. She was sorely tempted to let her mother continue without her, but the habit of following her mother—not to mention her lack of other choices—won out. Within the hour they had left the forests behind them, and began winding their way through a pass at the base of the Impossible Mountains. At first the pass meandered like a slow-moving river, but as the mountains rose up around them, the pass tucked into the belly of one of the mountains, and then rose like a lapping tongue into a waiting maw suspended between the peaks. Boselmia gasped when she saw it.

"*Ootholo Igwe*," Maisa said. Massaporan for "Black Riddle."

The mouth of the cave was a monstrous, magnificent thing. It hung on the side of the mountain like a doorway to a world that warned not to be entered but whose pull is too strong to resist. Daggers of rock climbed the cave's entranceway like jagged teeth, and its mouth was darker than the blackest night. But the cave wasn't entirely off-putting. Even from afar, Boselmia sensed its appeal, the way it tempted travelers to come close. Boselmia knew the legends surrounding the Black Riddle, both the Massaporan and the Jindois versions, and she knew bits and pieces of Maisa's descension into its void years ago. If they were here, it was for one reason and one reason only.

Maisa was ready for Boselmia to take her first steps toward becoming the *Fecheholo*.

They drew closer. Waiting for them near the mouth of a cave was a man. He was long and lean of both body and face. Although Boselmia had seen him only a couple of months ago, she scarcely recognized him. Prala. Her younger half-brother. He had the look of a warrior now, one who had known battle. Boselmia assumed that Prala was loyal to Wolfresh, his father, so seeing him here jarred her in a most unexpected way.

"Is he on our side?" Boselmia asked her mother, uncertain.

"Of course. Prala has always recognized what is most important," Maisa replied. The *Fecheholo's* eyes were full of love for her son. Boselmia wondered where along the line she had failed to notice that her half-brother was closer to their mother than she was.

Prala greeted them bearing a deerskin bag carrying an unspecified object. He nodded warily at Boselmia, as if confused by her presence. He presented the bag to Maisa with the solemnity of one handing over something sacred.

"I did as you asked," he said. He opened up the bag and revealed a sphere of pure light. It looked like the sun in miniature, only clearer, cleaner. "Everything was as you said it would be."

"Is that…" Boselmia began, but Maisa finished the sentence for her.

"*Cheyesh. Funato's* eternal light. Prala retrieved it for me. Without it, we would be lost, without hope. As would the Massaporan people. But now—now there is still a way."

Prala didn't respond. It was clear that he had been through a difficult trial, although he tried hard not to show it.

Maisa smiled, a careworn expression. "My children," she said. She reached out and brought the three of them together under the raven-feathered cloak, a conference of skulls. "In so many ways I have failed you. But, as is always the case with failure, one must use it to prepare for victory further down the line. Yestric, my son, our *Dachahelu*, may live and drive the Harrish off Tsadanali, or he may die. If he lives, he'll forever answer to Wolfresh, who will never allow him to rule the way the *Dachahelu* should. His waking dream would be full of shadows, and the Massaporan people's would as well. But I fear that Yestric's days are numbered. Strong though he is, he needs my guidance to defeat the Harrish in full, and I am no longer with him. I also doubt that Wolfresh wants Yestric to survive until the end of the war. Win or lose, Wolfresh means to rule. And he can only rule the Massaporan people if there is no *Dachahelu*."

She paused, looking at her two children in turn. "But I have a different plan. If Yestric dies, as I expect him to, I will bring Boselmia's unborn child into the world as the new *Dachahelu*."

She paused again, and as she did so, she stood back from them and looked south, her outstretched arms following her eyes. "Doido is coming for us. Maybe not today, maybe not tomorrow, but someday in the future, he will try to end our lives. Fortunately, *Ootholo Igwe* contains all of the knowledge in the universe, if one is strong enough to survive its trials." She turned to Boselmia. "You and I will not emerge from the Black Riddle until it teaches us how to see those who sing the Keebro song. By then you will have learned the language of creation that stirs in my blood, the language that a true *Fechebolo* speaks. But first, you must make the decision to enter the Black Riddle with me. The choice is your own."

Before Boselmia could answer, Maisa turned to Prala. "You must go into hiding."

"Where?"

"Deep into the mountains. For a time. Stay close to where you found *Funato's* eternal light. If you sense trouble, hide there. When we re-emerge from *Ootholo Igwe*, the three of us will live together. As a family. We will protect each other and, when Boselmia's child is born, we will protect the new *Dachahelu*. And then, when the time is right, we will return and end Wolfresh's rule."

Boselmia took a deep breath. The Black Riddle beckoned. She had always known that fate would bring her here, in the form of her mother. But, for the moment at least, the choice of whether or not to enter was still hers. She closed her eyes and imagined spurning Maisa, turning around and heading southeast. She might return to the bottom of the lake of the poured night sky. She might die there. It would be a freedom of sorts. A freedom that was entirely hers.

She opened her eyes. Her mother was staring at her, her face hardened by the difficult choices she had made over the years, the black spill of raven feathers covering her body like a shadowy cloud. Boselmia soaked in Maisa's attention, holding her answer like the edge of a knife.

"I'm ready," she said.

7

199 A.D.

When at first she awoke, she was so disoriented and confused that she was unable to remember who she was or where she was. She moved to her hands and knees, and from there was confronted with the sight of Etu and Aagili's corpses: one bisected cleanly in half, and the other charred to naught. There were sights that she had seen long ago in the Black Riddle that haunted her still, and for a moment she was convinced that she was in *Ootholo Igwe* again, trying to bridge the gap between the horrors and the wonders of creation. But no. This was different. The memory of those who should have been present but weren't flooded back in a rush. The traitor Doido's son—Doshensa of the *Koeceti*. And the boy, the *Dachahelu*—Notel.

Her head was a thunderstorm. She sat back down and tried to focus on what was most important. She considered using the *jwonatuwe* to tend to her wounds, but when she attempted to summon magic, it was beyond her reach. Her exhausted body begged her to stop. She rolled over and collapsed, surrendering to the fatigue, to the pain. But then out of the thunderstorm cracked a lightning bolt of thought. *Doido's pebble.* She moved her hands to the inside of the raven-feathered cloak, seeking, searching, body and mind trying to work in concert, but coming up empty.

The stone was missing.

Reality set in. The *Dachahelu* was gone, and she had no means of finding him.

She felt nauseous. Sleepy. Black bile churned in her distressed depths, black thoughts plagued her brain. She considered surrendering to the undertow, but the question of the missing stone kept her awake. Had the boy stolen it? It had to have been either him or Doshensa. She had thought Doshensa dead, but where was his corpse? Had he survived, and then stolen both the *Dachahelu* and the stone? Her memories of the moments before she went unconscious were a muddy river. Who had knocked her out? She dredged the banks of her subconscious, to no avail.

She knew that she needed to stand up, to move, or she would fall asleep again. She recalled visiting Ayyit earlier that day in the

Massaporan burial ground. *If I can drag myself back to her grave, I can fall in and be done with it,* she thought. She smiled on the inside. Thinking about death always made her feel a little better.

She summoned all of her energy, and pulled herself to her feet. Once upright, a savage host of wild, broken thoughts rushed up at her. *If the boy is lost, death is the only cure. Without him…* She remembered her mother's last words to her decades before, the day Maisa left to split the world in two. "*Ootholo Igwe* showed me a vision. The chamber of destruction bled into the chamber of creation and I knew. The next *Dachahelu* will be the last. He will destroy all of our enemies. Only make certain that he reaches adulthood. The sacrifice that I intend to make, you must be prepared to make as well." She had been prepared for years to make that sacrifice. She would gladly give her life, but losing the boy was different…she imagined her mother waiting for her in *iiwase,* hounding her for all of eternity, death becoming not the release she had hoped for but instead a doorway to a state where her failings as the *Fecheholo* resounded for forever and ever. The other *Fecheholos* would join in as well. She envisioned Bo, her namesake, waiting to heap on the abuse. Massaporan legend claimed that Bo was as strong as ten men, and as fierce as twenty. Boselmia knew that Bo would never allow her to spend eternity peaceably with Ayyit, not if she had lost the boy.

There was no point in dying. Death would be just as miserable as life.

Boselmia stumbled forward. The forest was a maze, but the moss-covered trees pointed the way out. *North,* she convinced herself. *He would go north, toward Ootholo Igwe.* She started north, but after a moment the futility of her mission struck her. She was an old woman, searching after a god with ever-growing physical powers. Without Doido's pebble to guide her, she was lost.

She sat back down. Tried to clear her head. But the storm kept raging, an unforgiving maelstrom. She didn't know where to go. She didn't know what to do.

She was the *Fecheholo*, the Raven Queen. Protector of the Deer King, the *Dachahelu.*

And she had lost him.

8

176 A.D.

She cried for days after Riiyisti died. She had been strong for so long, just as her mother had commanded, and it had all been for naught. Her son, the *Dachahelu*, was dead.

The villagers thought her mad. They had ample reason. She rent her buckskin dress and refused to wear another, electing instead to walk around looking obscene, uncaring that her female body spilled out of the ragged strips of clothing. She smeared ash and dirt on her face and arms. When the rains came and washed her clean, she immediately sullied herself again. She sat cross-legged for hours at a time repeating Riiyisti's name—as a monotone drone, as a prayer, as an unceasing scream. When the villagers tried to console her, she summoned the *jwonatuwe* and gave them a small taste of the terrible magic that haunted her veins, until they left her alone in her grief. She nearly used the *jwonatuwe* when her nine-year-old daughter Shayo tried to console her, but she stopped herself at the last moment, screaming at Shayo to leave her alone instead.

She was all the more grief-stricken because she had known for years that this was how it would end. Riiyisti had been both stubborn and needy as a boy, and she had never found the proper balance between nurturing him and doing the difficult work of transforming him into a war god. She spent his childhood lurching between the extremes, and then, when she invariably lost control, she fell back, time and again, on the words from the old tongue that brought him to heel. By the time he was sixteen, the words no longer had an effect. Every day since, she had lived in fear of the inevitable: the day that he would die.

And now that day had come to pass.

She had been in mourning for a fortnight when the *Fecheholo* returned. When Maisa saw Boselmia, she joined her on the ground, sitting cross-legged without word or comment. Hours passed. The longer Maisa sat there, the more difficult it was for Boselmia to hold on to her grief; rage took its place, a blinding, white-hot fury that steadily built into a paroxysm of hate.

"Leave me!" she screamed at last, unable to bear her mother's presence a moment longer. In her madness, she tore clumps of chalky black hair from her scalp. Despite all of this, the *Fecheholo* refused to leave. Boselmia, frustrated, started a manic chant, "Leave me! Leave me! Leave me! Leave—"

Maisa shot out her hands and grabbed Boselmia. The air left Boselmia's lungs suddenly, as, for the first time in her life, she was accosted with the black magic that ran through both her and her mother's veins. She tried to respond in kind, but her own *jwonatuwe* was a pale imitation of Maisa's; and so she surrendered, helpless in the *Fecheholo's* grasp. As she sat there, comatose, her mind drifted into the foggy sea of her time in *Ootholo Igwe* eighteen years earlier: she remembered the way Maisa had looked standing inside of the chamber of destruction, the way her power had grown with each implausible second that she endured the chamber's horrors. Boselmia, whose own stint in the chamber had scarcely begun before she succumbed to the pain, watched in awe, captivated by her mother's resolve. She had known then, as she knew now, that she could never hope to match her mother's strength.

When the last of Boselmia's resistance faded, Maisa released her. Boselmia felt Maisa's *jwonatuwe* retreating like a receding tide, leaving her with only her own meager portion, a puddle after a passing storm. Bereft of all joy, she looked at her mother, to see what she had to say.

"The time for mourning is over."

It wasn't what Boselmia wanted to hear. "I failed him. Not you. That means I'm the one who will decide when the mourning is done," she spat.

Maisa, the black-feather cloak hanging about her shoulders like a cascade of black ice, remained expressionless. "Life is full of failure. Yestric's failure. Riiyisti's failure. Our failures. But it doesn't change what we have to do. We are meant to return our people to the *Dachahelu's* waking dream. And it's time we get back to work."

"I am not the *Fecheholo*. You are. Do what you like."

Maisa was quiet for a long time. Boselmia thought perhaps that she had at long last convinced Maisa of her unsuitability as a divinity. But when her mother spoke, she realized how wrong she was. "I mean to die soon. And in my death, I intend to deal the Harrish a blow from which they will never recover. After I'm gone, you will bring another *Dachahelu* into the world, the *Dachahelu* who will return our people to his waking dream."

Boselmia laughed. "You're mad. Why should the next *Dachahelu's* fate be any different than Riiyisti's? Than Yestric's?"

"Because I saw what would happen all those years ago in *Ootholo Igwe*. After I'm gone, you will bring another *Dachahelu* into the world. He will be Notel, the second *Dachahelu*, come again. He will be the last *Dachahelu*. Only make certain that he reaches adulthood. The sacrifice that I intend to make, you must be prepared to make as well." Her voice grew distant, faraway. Combined with the raven-feather cloak, she appeared on the verge of slipping into another dimension. "Through him you will succeed where I have failed."

Boselmia's heart nearly stopped. She felt faint with what she thought at first was anger, but soon realized was relief.

"You knew? Even before Riiyisti was born, you knew that he would die?"

"Yes."

Boselmia's head spun. Was her mother lying to her? For years she had suffered alone, shouldering the burden of Riiyisti's shortcomings, growing ever more certain of his eventual failure, and now her mother was telling her that Riiyisti's fate had been writ in the heart of the Black Riddle long before.

Maisa grabbed Boselmia hard about the shoulders. Forced Boselmia to look her in the eye. "Do you hear me, my one and only daughter? You must press on. Will you do what our people need you to do?" A renegade tear worked its way down Maisa's cheek as she spoke, as out of place as a snowflake in an inferno.

Boselmia nodded yes.

Maisa sighed, relieved. She released Boselmia and looked at her from an arm's length. "Good. I swear that what I have told you will come to pass. But first—" and here she sighed again, only this time it was a different sort of sigh, an exhalation doubling as a precursor to the unexpected, "—you must go south and make a peace."

Later that night, after hours spent talking with her mother, Boselmia stole away from the village and took a dip in the lake of the poured night sky. She hadn't been in the lake since her flirtation with death years ago, but this time there was no draw to the suicidal impulse, only a focus on washing away the last of her sorrow. It worked. The water cleansed her with a cool indifference to past sins, interested only in its present work. After a time, Boselmia felt whole.

She was emerging from the lake when she spotted a leonine shadow in the rushes. She knew who it was even in the darkness.

Jueshwella.

Boselmia pretended to pay her no mind. She stood naked on the grassy bank, drying off in the cool night air. Jueshwella walked toward her. They had avoided each other since Shayo's birth, although their lives remained intertwined: though infrequent, there were still nights when Cayap visited Boselmia's cabin, and, despite her distaste for the man and his desires, Boselmia always let him do as he pleased, in the hopes that Jueshwella would learn about it and feel pain.

Jueshwella stopped ten feet away. Jueshwella had long been frightened of Boselmia's powers, but she had something to say, and it was clear she meant to say it.

When she spoke, it was with a soft, trembling voice. "You are an ugly woman. You always have been."

It was true. Boselmia had never been pretty, and now, nearing fifty, her physical flaws had hardened: she had large, coarse hands and an asymmetrical, tree-sprig nose and dirty brown eyes that burrowed into a deep-pocketed face. She looked more like her mother than her long-dead father, but whereas her mother's looks were made secondary by her dignity and strength, Boselmia's demanded one's foremost attention.

Jueshwella crept closer. The moonlight tried to catch her still-lustrous brown hair in a silvery web, but the flow slipped through, as effortless as a waterfall through a net.

"Worse, you're a disgrace to our people," Jueshwella continued. "I wasn't surprised when I heard that a Torquecan slave slit your son's throat like he was a common pig. You were supposed to give birth to a warrior-god but instead you gave us a weakling. Now our people are doomed."

The *jwonatuwe* stirred in Boselmia's blood, but she tempered it back down, refusing to be provoked. Though it seemed a childish urge, what she really wanted was to grab Jueshwella by the hair and kiss her, the way they had kissed years ago. Everything between them had been a lie even back then, but knowing it was a lie didn't make Boselmia want Jueshwella any less.

A realization dawned on Boselmia. She said, "Your sons are dead, aren't they?" Jueshwella's boys had followed Riiyisti south, and then west, touched by *iiwase*, which meant they were almost certainly dead; perhaps their scalps now hung from an Effanarem warrior's belt, or their bodies were plugged with Harrish shot, or their necks had been wrung by a Breekish mercenary, or, like Riiyisti, perhaps a former Torquecan slave had slit their throats.

Jueshwella gasp-sobbed, then quickly stopped, choking down her pain. When she opened her mouth, poison spilled out, heavy and hot. "You are a whore, a destroyer of life, a conniving demon-spawn who would kill us all. I hope you and your mother meet your fates at the hands of the Harrish, or better, I hope that Doido Mass finishes the job before the Harrish get the chance. I rue the day my husband and my husband's father before him were fooled into believing that the *Fecheholo* was the answer to our people's prayers. I hope your mother dies. I hope you die. I hope your bastard daughter dies. But before that, I hope you suffer. As you have made me suffer."

She knew then that her intuition was right: Jueshwella's sons were dead. But there was more to it than that.

"Why are you here?"

Jueshwella softened. The softening was almost imperceptible, but it was there, at the edges. "I didn't come here to find you, if that's what you're asking. This place was my home long before you and your mother claimed it like stray dogs. This lake was my lake long before you dipped your saggy ass in its waters." She stargazed as she spoke, her faraway eyes suggesting that she was trying to mount a defense of her own mind.

Boselmia, however, sensed the truth of what Jueshwella was up to; its chill spread like a deep frost through her bones, working its way toward her heart. Knowing pained her, but what pained her more was knowing that she couldn't change what Jueshwella had planned; that, in fact, any effort made on her behalf to stop Jueshwella would likely only cause Jueshwella to double her efforts.

"I loved you, once," she said, trying.

"You love me now. Why else would you let my husband into your bed, if not to get close to me? But know this: I never loved you. Were you not the *Fecheholo's* daughter, I would have never given you a second thought. You are unlovable. Unloved. For now and always. By everything and everyone."

They held a silence between them that was ugly at first, then sacred, then meaningless. On the other side of the lake, a heron sounded a raspy note. All around, the deepening darkness accrued more definition.

At last Jueshwella turned and walked away. Down the bank and into the water. She took slow, steady steps that sent languorous ripples out into the moonlit waters. The lake climbed her body with patience but without apology. When it swallowed her head, it said not a word.

In the morning, Maisa said her goodbyes. The village—that loyal northern bastion of *Fecheholo* worship—gathered to send their deity away, a deity who had only yesterday returned.

Her message was blunt. "You will not see me again. Boselmia is the *Fecheholo* now." In front of a population decimated due to the failings of Boselmia's son, Maisa robed Boselmia with the raven-feathered cloak. When she put the cloak around Boselmia's shoulders, the quartz-white sky opened and spat at them. If it was an omen, it was difficult to tell what it meant: the rain stopped as soon as it had begun.

"Go south *now*," Maisa said, pulling Boselmia close. "Keep Prala by your side. Make peace and mean it. Then leave. You'll know I'm dead when the tales of what I have done start to spread. They may come for you then. But they'll have no heart for it. Except Doido. The day approaches when you'll have to kill him. Do it before he kills you."

Minutes later, Maisa left on a dapple-gray, moving southeast at a snail's pace, looking old and harmless. Boselmia watched her mother go with the rest of the village, thinking that she ought to feel sadness, or joy. But she felt nothing.

Soon after, it was her turn to say goodbye. The villagers, who had gathered out of respect for Maisa, were already dissipating; it was clear they cared for one *Fecheholo* and one *Fecheholo* only. Shortly, the only ones who remained were Prala, Cayap, and Shayo. The men stared at Boselmia, waiting, while Shayo lingered in the shadows of a dew oak, watching her mother while pretending not to.

Boselmia approached Cayap. He wore white breeches braided with a blue-and-gold beaded belt, a hunting shirt that left his torso exposed, and a soft scowl. Boselmia assumed he didn't know that his wife was dead. When she opened her mouth, she discovered that she was eager to break the news.

"Your pretty wife is at the bottom of the lake. I saw her walk into the waters myself."

Cayap's scowl deepened, but he said nothing.

His tepid reaction excited her. A metallic taste pooled in the corners of her mouth. "Do you believe me?"

"Yes," he admitted after some effort. He gave the smallest of shrugs. "What is done is done."

"Your husbandly devotion is touching," she said, hoping to hurt him. She paused, gave him a cock-eyed grin. "Dead sons. A dead wife. All that's left of your legacy is a string-bean girl with bad blood. You'll look after Shayo while I'm gone, won't you?"

"She is my daughter," he replied by way of a *yes*. "And I chose long ago to serve the *Fecheholo*. Nothing else matters."

"You fucked the *Fecheholo* is what you did. And I let you. Because I wanted to hurt your dead wife. But I never wanted you. You should know that."

This brought a smirking smile to Cayap's face. "I was referencing the real *Fecheholo*—your mother. And I couldn't care less what you wanted. Now go die your stupid death at the hands of our enemies, and in doing so free me of my curse."

She laid a hand on him. The *jwonatuwe* stirred in her blood, warming the ends of her fingertips. "I should kill you. Leave you in the lake with your wife." *Perhaps I'll even join you at the bottom*, she thought, momentarily crazed again, but even as she thought it, she knew that she would not be welcome in that watery grave.

He shrugged again, this time a mountainous roll of the shoulders. "Do what you want. Everything I've worked for is destroyed. Because of you."

She saw it then—the pain in his face flickering to the surface. It jarred her back to reality. She removed her hand and scrambled away from Cayap, toward Prala.

"Let's go," she said when she reached her brother. He nodded, and they started walking. Her thoughts were muddy, disorganized, but a mosquito bite of memory drew her attention toward the tree line, where Shayo was standing, watching her leave. Seeing her daughter satisfied the itch. She put Cayap's village behind her, and walked south.

Everywhere was devastation. From the west, the survivors were still in retreat, fresh tales on their lips of Effanarem war parties pursuing Massaporans deep into Wolfresh territory, past even the eastern reaches of the Yipikurri. From the south, the stories were no less terrifying: a massive Harrish army had gathered at the Havenese border, and were readying to deal a fatal blow to the Massaporan nation. But on Boselmia walked, ever south, into the teeth of her people's fears. There, Wolfresh and Doido Mass and unknown others waited, ostensibly to strike an accord.

The *Jaironim* Woods grew deeper as she walked, entangling Boselmia in the heart of Wolfresh. She walked past towering dew oaks that hid their faces on high; past blood elms with intersecting ridges of bark that pulsed red near the root system; past supple jorkwood trees that seemed to bow in obeisance to their hardwood betters; and, once or twice, past wiswake trees, those chimerical oddities of the forest, flaunting their medicinal powers by way of their silvery-purple bark. Boselmia was a *Toway* girl, always had been, and never knew quite what to make of the *Jaironim* Woods: it was a land with a dark, unknowable heart, a heart beating somewhere in its sprawling sternum of limbs, in time to the dying hopes of the Massaporan people.

She knew that they were close when the woods began to change. The dew oaks gave way to white poplars, elms, and birch. Other differences were also evident. Once whistling winds started whispering, as if in fear, and sightings of their fellow Massaporans dwindled to zero. No one, it seemed, dared travel this close to the border. A couple of times Boselmia stopped and sniffed the wind, thinking she could smell the Harrish on the breeze. But still Prala led them on, twisting and turning through ever-thinning copses until they came upon a clearing on the precipice of a small rise. There the principals were waiting, in a makeshift campsite marked by the shelters of three different nations: the Massaporan lean-to, the Effanarem tipi, and the Harrish pavilion.

A Harrishman emerged from the pavilion. He was a sizeable creature, with sharp green eyes that stared at Boselmia and Prala in a way that suggested he knew who they were. On the top of his head and around the borderlands of his mouth grew tufts of dirty blond hair. Boselmia hadn't seen a Harrishman since she was a girl fleeing *Toway* with her mother. This one struck her as more exotic than she remembered.

The Harrishman said nothing, but his eyes trailed to the tipi, signaling. From the opposite side of the tipi stepped a gnarled tree of a man, old beyond comprehension—Hiata Oxaway, the great chief of the Effanarem people. Trailing after him came a younger, tougher-looking figure, whose head was shaven except for a bold strip of tufted brown down the middle. If the tipi and their respective appearances didn't make it clear that they were Effanarem, the haughty look of recent victory on their faces left no doubt.

She looked to the lean-to, waiting for Wolfresh and Doido to emerge. But they were nowhere to be seen. Then Prala harrumphed, and nodded to his left. Boselmia followed his gaze and found Wolfresh cresting the rise, a string of fresh-caught bass in hand. Behind him trailed Doido, a mess of wild black hair bunching around skin-and-bone shoulders. Though Wolfresh was the head of the Massaporan nation, it was the skinny Doido that Boselmia feared: three times in her life she had seen Doido's skeletal form emerge from an ash-gray cloud, death in the offing. She had survived each encounter, but the next time he snuck up on her, she knew she'd have to face him alone.

Wolfresh saw her. "The daughter," he said in the Massaporan tongue. He looked and sounded disappointed. Boselmia glanced at the others. Besides the four Massaporans present, it appeared the only other person who understood what Wolfresh had said was the younger Effanarem.

A second Harrishman emerged from the pavilion, in his fifties perhaps, prosaic in every way. He stood dully in the blond-haired man's shadow.

"The *Fecheholo*," Boselmia responded, correcting Wolfresh. "But perhaps in your old age you've grown blind, and cannot see my cloak."

"I see your feathers," he said. "They do not make you the *Fecheholo*."

The blond-haired Harrishman interrupted their repartee with a booming voice. "Speak Harrish," he commanded.

Boselmia knew how to speak Harrish: Prala was fluent, and he had worked with her for years until she, too, had mastered the tongue. But she wasn't about to start the negotiations by giving in to the Harrishman's first demand. She continued addressing Wolfresh in Massaporan as if the blond-haired man hadn't spoken. "Perhaps a demonstration of my powers would satisfy you. Come closer, and I'll give you and that long-haired rat behind you a taste."

Wolfresh's expression didn't change as he replied, "That's not necessary. As for calling yourself the *Fecheholo*: if you're determined to play the part, I hope you play it well. The Harrish need to leave believing that they've spoken with the deity."

"That's exactly what they'll be doing. But by all means, let's clear this up." Boselmia turned her attention to the blond-haired Harrishman. She decided that if the Harrish language was where they were heading, she might as well beat Wolfresh to the punch. "My mother, the old *Fecheholo*, is dead," she proclaimed in the Harrish tongue. "I am the new *Fecheholo*. Long live the *Fecheholo*." She finished with a wry, magnificent smile.

The blond-haired man parted his teeth for her in turn. A swift and beastly smile. "As you say," he replied. "We have long heard that the mother had a daughter. For my sake and yours, I hope you're telling the truth. My name is Daniel Redgrave, Olgard ambassador to the indigenous nations of Wolfresh and Oxaway. My associate is Mathias Potter, brother of Brigand Potter, the hero who put the previous Deer King in the ground. From what I've heard, a former Torquecan slave had the honors this time around."

His words made Boselmia's anger stir, and her heart ache. She tried disguising her feelings with a biting voice. "Ambassador, you say? You're off to a poor start for a man versed in diplomacy. After that disrespect, I'd sooner kill you than negotiate."

"You mistake my intentions, Raven Queen. I'd love for nothing more than to leave here with a justification for all-out war."

"If you're fortunate enough to leave, you cur, it will be because I'm content with the agreement we've reached. Not because you are."

The threat hung in the air like static before a thunderstorm. Wolfresh rushed in to discharge it. "The *Fecheholo* is here because she recognizes that the time for peace has come. And our Harrish and Effanarem friends are here because they understand that the *Fecheholo* has access to a deep and powerful magic that she will not hesitate to use to save her people. A magic that can be used time and time again. A magic that must be put to rest if we are ever to have peace."

She had never wanted to kill Wolfresh more. But her mother's words rang in her ears: *Make a peace. Whatever the terms, make a peace. If you don't, they'll kill us all. But give me time, and I'll multiply their troubles tenfold. Then our opportunity will arise once more.*

She kept her mouth shut.

A silence masquerading as peace descended. With tired arms, Wolfresh carried the string of bass over to the fire. Soon the men had their knives out, scaling and cleaning the fish. Even the dull-looking Mathias Potter joined in, going about the task with the mechanical industry that Boselmia had long associated with the Harrish people. She watched and wondered if Mathias's brother, Brigand, had gone about killing Yestric with the same stupid diligence.

The group dined on the bass under a gentle midafternoon sun. The silence, which bore on and on, took on a contented quality, and for a time, it seemed that all issues between the parties might be resolved in the midst of this great calm. But when the last of the food was eaten, Daniel Redgrave spoke.

"Damn, that was tasty. You will never hear me say that you people don't know how to prepare fish. Perhaps in another life I was born a Massaporan, to have such an appreciation. But enough of that." He turned to Wolfresh. "Tell me, Wolfresh, why the great chief Oxaway and I should spare your little nation, when you cannot control the dark magic this woman works? You swore eighteen years ago that neither the Raven Queen nor the Deer King would threaten our people again. You swore that once the Raven

Queen was dead, no Deer King could be reborn. But now thousands have died at a new Deer King's hand, and I sit in parley with one of the witches you promised to kill."

Wolfresh started to reply, but Boselmia beat him to the punch. "To Wolfresh's credit, he did try!" she cackled. "He sent that rat-haired skeleton beside him to do the job, but my mother spanked Cloudworm on the ass and sent him on his way."

It was more or less the truth. Years ago, shortly after Boselmia and her mother had emerged from *Ootholo Igwe,* Doido launched his attack. Maisa, who along with Boselmia had spent her time inside the Black Riddle learning to anticipate Keebro magic, sensed what was coming. She was waiting for Doido when he emerged from his cloud, and she nearly killed him, but he squirmed back into the cloud as quickly as he had appeared, looking like a frantic, tunneling worm. Boselmia had referred to him as Cloudworm ever since, although this was the first chance she had had to do it in person.

Daniel Redgrave laughed. "Cloudworm! I like that! I've seen his disappearing tricks too. It's a fitting description."

Doido sat stone-faced, refusing to respond to the indignity with a reaction.

Wolfresh stepped in. "It's true. We failed. The Raven Queen was too strong. But now Doido has taken her power out of the equation." Wolfresh turned to his protégé. "Show them."

Doido stood. Only then did Boselmia notice how tired and haggard he looked. She thought that there was something familiar about his exhaustion, especially the way he hid it behind a resolute expression and dogged eyes. His was the exhausted look of a saint, one who had survived the journey to hell and back. One who...

No. It's not possible. He couldn't have.

Doido reached into a pocket hidden inside his buckskin leggings, and pulled out two blue-gray stones. For the briefest of moments he considered them in his palm, as if bemused by their nature, before holding them aloft for the others to see. No one knew what to make of them, save for Chief Oxaway, who laughed an old man's brittle laugh.

Boselmia turned cold. *He's been inside. The same as us.*

The next words out of Doido's mouth confirmed her fears. "Funatan Stones. From *Ootholo Igwe.*"

"*Ootholo Igwe?*" asked Daniel Redgrave.

"It translates to Black Riddle in your tongue. It's a sacred cave to both the Effanarem and the Massaporan people."

"And where is this cave found?"

Doido hesitated. But only for a second. "At the base of the Impossible Mountains, north of Wolfresh. Long ago, before even the arrival of the Torquec in Tsadanali, the Massaporan, Effanarem, and Keebro were one people—the Jindois. The Jindois believed that all of creation derives from *Ootholo Igwe*."

"You were once one people?" an incredulous Redgrave asked.

"Many years ago. Yes," responded Doido. Chief Oxaway gave a curt, affirming nod.

It was obvious that Redgrave was curious, but he pressed on. "And what do these stones do?"

"These stones were washed in *Funato's* eternal spring, deep in *Ootholo Igwe's* belly. Ask the stones the *Dachahelu's* true name and they'll show where he resides. Even if he is still in the womb. Ask the stones again and they'll take you to him. With these stones the *Fecheholo* will never be able to hide *Dachahelu* again. You…we…can kill him the instant he's born."

A panic rose in Boselmia's chest. *You swore, Mother. You swore that I would bring another Dachahelu into the world. He would be the one…* The memories of Maisa's many false proclamations washed over Boselmia like a tidal wave surging up from The Orphan's Mouth. Had Maisa told yet another lie? Was this yet another false trail destined to end in disaster?

A voice, from beside her. "You betray our people." It was Prala, Boselmia's dear sweet half-brother, leveling the accusation at his cousin. Boselmia had nearly forgotten he was there.

Doido whipped his stringy black hair at his cousin, his tongue like a blade. "Our people are nearly extinct because dead and dying gods keep leading them to the grave."

"And you would have us worship who? *Funato*? Would you make us Effanarem? Tell me: how did you find your way inside *Ootholo Igwe*? What heathen magic are you using now?"

Doido sidestepped the question. "This from the brother of a woman who reanimates the corpse of a long-dead god over and over again, only to watch him hurry back to the grave the moment he reaches maturity."

"Silence!" thundered Wolfresh. The force of his bellow was so strong that it startled everyone present, including the Harrish. "These are petty Massaporan disputes, disputes that must be settled at another time. The reason we are here today is to make a peace. A permanent peace that can only be bought with the assurance that the *Dachahelu* will never rise again."

Wolfresh reached out his hand to Doido. Doido handed over the stones. In turn, Wolfresh gave the blue-gray rocks to Daniel Redgrave. "Eighteen years ago, I vouched to the Harrish people that the *Dachahelu* would not return. But I failed in that promise. Today, we offer this gift in the hopes that the Harrish will see fit to prevent such an occurrence themselves. And then we humbly pray that they will spare us our lives, and, if they see fit, our land."

The panic in Boselmia's chest took flight like a murmuration of starlings. She reached for the *jwonatuwe*, but it was far away, lost in the undulating swell of emotion commandeering her system. She needed to take action, needed to kill, needed to steal the stones and take them with her so that she could fulfill her mother's legacy, only she knew it might not be sufficient; there were too many of them, and her mother had told her, *no,* commanded her…

"*Fechebolo.*"

It was the dull-looking man who spoke—Mathias Potter, the brother of the Harrish hero who had once struck down Yestric. Only now he didn't look quite so dull: his hazel eyes crackled with a powerful energy, the fire of kept secrets. To her surprise, the others went quiet, deferring to this small, common-looking man. He opened his mouth to speak to her, and the world went still.

"I came all the way here to see you. You or your mother, I suppose. In my dreams, there are always two ravens, circling high above, and a third, far-off, calling. Your mother isn't dead yet, is she? No, not yet. But you are the *Fechebolo* now. That much is true."

His voice centered her. She corralled her will, pooled the *jwonatuwe* in her fingers. "You're not who you say you are."

He smiled as a streak of green flashed across his eyes. "I haven't been this far west in many years. I was afraid to return. The *Dachahelu* was the one who died, but I've paid the price in other ways. It's a terrible thing, being haunted by a god."

"You're Brigand. Not Mathias."

"Perhaps. Brigand and Mathias Potter are identical twins, one and the same. Or they were, until the day one of them murdered a deity."

He is Brigand. She studied her long-dead brother's killer. He studied her back. Worlds of space and time passed between them. She saw Yestric's glory deep inside his eyes, the way that her brother had won a convert at the very end. She saw that his common features were a disguise. The *jwonatuwe* cooled. She understood.

"Say what you came to say," she said.

He didn't hesitate. "Swear that you will never bring the *Dachahelu* back to life. Then leave. Go north into the Impossible Mountains. Or better yet, go west, to the Atalagadu River on the far side of the continent, and cross over. Don't come back."

Everyone else heard it as a command. She heard it as a warning. Unspoken words trailed in the wake: *For a time, dear Raven Queen. Only for a time.* She had never been more certain of anything.

He continued. "An agreement will be reached today that will not involve you in any way, shape, or form, although you must abide by it. Two miles south, an army stands poised to wipe the Massaporan people off the face of the earth. But Brigand Potter is a hero to his people, and that hero has made a request. Spare the Massaporan people, and spare their land. The nation of Olgard wants the *Fecheholo* dead, but I know from what Wolfresh and Doido Mass have told us that the Raven Queen is not so easily killed. My friend Redgrave here would nevertheless love to make an attempt, as would those back in Centichester, but, for today at least, it is my decision that matters. What I need to know, *Fecheholo,* is whether you will do as I have asked?"

"I will," she said.

In an instant, the fire died in Brigand's eyes, and he became Mathias Potter once more. Wolfish faces re-entered the frame, snarling, threatening visages suggesting that the only pacts that would hold today were the ones made between the men. Boselmia settled on Doido Mass last.

"Our Harrish friends are generous," Doido said, staring at her with contempt. "Now leave as you were asked, so that we may make a new world without you in it."

Her tongue strained at the cave of her mouth, but she kept it entombed. When she stood, Prala rose with her. The wolves watched the two of them stand, and then turned away, resuming their wolfish business. Wolfresh addressed Daniel Redgrave and Chief Oxaway in baritone, his words invoking the past to create a new present: "Long ago, when the Jindois were one people, a council of seven male chieftains was authorized to speak and make decisions on behalf of the nation. They were called the *Koeceti*…"

She listened as she left, the sounds of the past rushing in to destroy the dreams of every *Fecheholo* who had ever lived.

She was supposed to go north to the Impossible Mountains. Or west across the Atalagadu. She did neither. She walked north into *Jaironim*, and waited. She knew that she had made a promise to Brigand Potter, but she didn't care. Brigand was Harrish. *Iiwase* in his eyes or not, Brigand could hang.

A fortnight later, there came a morning when the sun rose black in the sky, cloaked in the shredded gauze of portentous clouds. *It's happened,* Boselmia thought, though what *it* was, she wasn't sure. For three straight days the sun rose like an obsidian stone, but then, on the fourth, the curse lifted, leaving Boselmia to wonder if the sign wasn't a sign at all. She went still and waited yet again: for another sign, for word of Maisa's miracle, for Doido, for some god other than her useless self to tell her what to do.

Weeks passed. Months maybe. She sent Prala away, to learn what he could. While he was gone, she subsisted on mushrooms and tree nuts, a creature of the forest. When she ran into her own people, she invariably lashed out at them, often using *jwonatuwe*. Doubt creeped in, and with it the latent hate she had for her mother surfaced once more. *Are you truly dead? If so, what good was your death? Did you die, like you lived, in vain?* Her frame of mind deteriorated. There were nights when she screamed into the blackness for Doido to come and take her. Other nights she would fall asleep and wake up thinking that she had returned to *Ootholo Igwe's* dark belly, only this time without Maisa. During the day, she resumed her conversation with her dead son. She was losing her mind, she was always losing her mind, where was her mother, she could never be the true *Fecheholo*, she was losing her *Funato*-cursed mind.

One day, a woman appeared. She was a lovely, timeworn thing, short in stature but fearless in nature, a fact made clear by the way she approached Boselmia without hesitation, unintimidated by the raven-feathered cloak. Boselmia was certain that she hated the woman the moment she saw her. She decided, as the woman approached, that she would send the woman to her grave. But when the woman reached Boselmia, she summoned a strange magic of her own: she touched Boselmia on the arm, and said "Come."

The woman led Boselmia to a little wooden house in the thick of the forest. Once there, she bade Boselmia to sleep on a straw bed. When Boselmia awoke, the woman fed her a proper meal—a squirrel and parsnips soup seasoned with basil—and then sat quietly as Boselmia supped. Throughout the meal, the woman didn't speak a word. The quiet that the woman carried with her was so powerful that Boselmia felt inclined to test the limits of it, and found, to her delight, that the spell still hadn't broken three days later.

By then Boselmia had fallen in love.

The woman's name was Ayyit. Eventually, they began talking to one another, although the conversations remained short affairs: Ayyit was naturally taciturn, and Boselmia, who had long ago developed the habit of using her tongue as a weapon, found that silence better suited her loving nature, a nature she had, up to that point, barely cultivated. Still, they managed to learn about one another. Ayyit was slightly older than Boselmia. She had lived on her own for most of her adult life, having elected long ago to eschew village living and its oppressive conventions. She had been married once, long ago, to an older man who had died fighting on the banks of the Yipikurri alongside Waisporek, Boselmia's father from another life.

Ayyit knew who Boselmia was, of course, and she didn't feign otherwise, which was a relief. "You're a god of our people. You must do what gods do."

Boselmia, still adrift in her soul, didn't pretend to know what being a god entailed. To her surprise, Ayyit was the one who showed her.

"You have enemies, don't you?" Ayyit asked one night in her spare, forthright way.

"Yes."

"Then you must be prepared to defeat them. Do not let me distract you from your purpose."

"But I want to be distracted. I want…you."

She hadn't spoken so baldly to another woman since her time with Jueshwella. She was sure that this situation was different, but once the words were spoken, she feared that she had misread Ayyit; she was no god, only a loveless, lovesick fool destined to go to her grave wanting. Her heart hammered in her chest as she waited for a reply.

Ayyit stepped forward and brushed Boselmia's graying hair back from her face. "And I want you. But we are old women, and know the ways of this world. Focus now. Defeat your enemies. Then we will take a moment for ourselves before the sun sets on our lives."

Ayyit's words were like a splash of cold water in the face. Immediately, Boselmia sensed the danger they were in, a danger brought on by her lovelorn state. Doido was coming.

She went outside. The stars hung high above like dangling knives, shiny and bright and threatening to fall. She placed a palm on the cold ground and asked Tsadanali to show her the seen and the unseen. The doors of perception parted, so that the dimensions next to Tsadanali's bled into the frame: *iiwase* and the gray lands and other that were mere pinpricks of light at the edge of the canvas of existence. But still no Doido. Not yet. But she sensed him: plotting, tracking, approaching.

She meditated on how to best stop Doido. Now that Doido had been inside *Ootholo Igwe*, Boselmia didn't know the extent of his powers. The Black Riddle was an enigma even to those who had plumbed its depths. Doido may have traveled the same path as Boselmia and her mother, giving him the power of *jwonatuwe*, or, in his searching for the Funatan Stones, he might have missed the chambers of creation and destruction entirely. It was possible that he had ventured down corridors that contained mysteries unknown even to Maisa, and now possessed powers greater than any *Fecheholo*. Even if not, he still knew the Keebro song that gave him entrance to the gray lands. At a minimum, she had to be prepared for him to attack her unawares.

Night turned to day. Boselmia kept at her prayer, hoping for answers. She thought of her mother, who she now knew in her heart was dead. As she thought of Maisa, she remembered the way her mother had stayed in a partially meditative state the first time they were waiting on Doido to attack. *Give me my mother's strength,* she prayed. The anger she had long felt toward her mother transformed into gratitude for all that Maisa had taught her. She held Maisa in that bountiful space the way one remembers a fond dream.

Day changed over into night. Words, images, and understandings came to her unbidden. Boselmia felt she was tapping into the divine, tapping into herself. She was tempted to grasp at the greater truths that existed just out of reach, but any attempt drove what wisdom she had acquired away; all she could do was sit and wait inside the fog of truth. She sat through yet another clear and cold night, the stars whispering strange intentions in the heavens above.

At daybreak, a moment of insight shook her like an internal earthquake.

Water.

She stood and walked south. After a half a mile, she reached the babbling stream where Ayyit drew freshwater. Boselmia was weak from fasting, but she knew that now wasn't the time to eat or drink. She sat behind an outcrop of rock overlooking the stream, and waited.

It wasn't long before Doido appeared. Boselmia had half-expected him to be traveling with a retinue, but no, he was alone. He looked thin and fierce, like the scarecrows the Harrish used in their fields out east, but also ragged, worn down by the pressures of life. For a moment, Boselmia imagined what it was like to be him: she saw the trials and tribulations she and her mother had put him through, how their very existence had undermined his worldview. She knew that he could never hope to bring about his vision for the Massaporan people so long as the *Fecheholo* lived.

As she watched, he knelt and drank water from the stream. He wore simple brown breeches and no shirt. Stringy black hair spilled over his shoulders like emaciated serpents slithering down a mountaintop. On his hip was a small deerskin bag.

When his gaze ran to the rocks, Boselmia took cover. Seconds later, she heard footsteps. She tried to stay hidden as he walked up the knoll, but there was nowhere to go.

Doido drew level with the rocks. Sensing something amiss, he turned in Boselmia's direction. His eyes went white with fury when he saw her. "You," he said.

"Me," she replied.

He was standing twenty yards away. She had few options at this distance, so she started to inch toward him. If he chose to sing the Keebro song, she wanted to be close enough to stop him before he slipped into the gray lands.

"You're a damned She-Devil," he spat. "And a liar. I knew your mother wasn't dead, although I imagine that's changed now. What she did—I can't imagine it cost her less than her life."

He knew. Whatever her mother had done, he knew what it was. What was more difficult to ascertain was how he felt about it.

She gave him her most wicked smile. "She said that she would deal the Harrish a blow from which they would never recover."

He laughed a sharp little laugh. "Maybe she did. She's given our people space, which is a gift. I won't deny it. But the story of our people's future is still to be written. You and I have been telling different versions of that story our entire lives. Now it's time to see whose version wins out."

She searched for the barbed rejoinder, the prying question, anything to keep him talking. There was so much that she needed to know: the extent of his powers; details of the hell that her mother had wrought; the easiest way to kill him. But she was deprived of those luxuries. Doido started moving toward her at a fast clip, his confidence underscored by the lack of a Keebro song on his lips.

Boselmia reached for the *jwonatuwe*. It came to her on the plane of readiness her mind had prepared for her these last two days. She was as powerful as she had ever been. A word from the old language swam to her tongue, a word fired in the heart of the chamber of destruction. She would kill him. She was sure of it.

But when he reached her, she found that he had a word of his own ready, an oceanic utterance that extinguished not only her word, but also the *jwonatuwe* in her blood. Instantly she was drowning in the spell that Doido's word had cast. Doido hovered far above the water line, holding her down while the life seeped from her being.

Hope deserted her. She saw the future writ in Doido's eyes, an endless line of male Massaporan chieftains with no *Fecheholo* and no *Dachahelu* to contend with, the *Dachahelu's* waking dream forgotten as the Harrish machine marched on. Doido's vision carved out a space for the old ways, but Boselmia saw the truth: in time, the Massaporan people would be subsumed and then consumed until, in effect, they existed no more.

Breathing became more difficult. As the air left her chest, even these understandings faded. *Iiwase* rose like a star into the gloaming of her existence. She was going to see her mother, much sooner than she had intended.

Only she didn't. Air bloomed in Boselmia's lungs, as Doido's lips suddenly formed an astonished O. She couldn't understand why, but the waters of Doido's spell were receding. As she pulled away from him, she saw the arrow sprouting from his chest. She gaped at Doido as the blood drained from his sorcerer's mask. At last he lost the battle to stay upright and slumped to the ground, dead.

Behind Doido stood Boselmia's brother, Prala, with a bow in hand.

Prala, long of face and short of words, replied with variations of the same explanation, no matter how many questions Boselmia asked.

"The sky went black on the eastern horizon for three straight days. Ever since, there have been no ships from the other side. They are calling it the Sundering. Torquecan slaves are already revolting. As for the Harrish, they are fighting among themselves, both in Tiderealm where the Whesker King rules, and in the lands where the Harrish claim to rule themselves. Some blame us, of course, but their problems are manifold now, and, at the present moment, they think us too weak to be a threat. There are still those who want to destroy us entirely, but the will is gone. If we are quiet for a time, if we hold to the Accord, our star will rise again."

The Sundering. Maisa had separated the Harrish from their source of power—the old world from which they had sprung. It was a victory almost beyond comprehension.

When Boselmia asked Prala to repeat himself for the fifth time, Ayyit hushed her. "No more," her lover said. "We have a body to bury."

There was a Massaporan burial ground nearby, but Boselmia wouldn't hear of it. They lugged Doido's body to a less honorable spot. Gave him a proper Harrish burial, deep in the dirt. Some rottenness spilled out of Boselmia's soul when they put him in the ground. "Lay there alone forever, you vile scum, you fucking traitor. Lay where no one will ever find you. Dream your Keebro dreams. Sleep your Harrish sleep. But know that you rot in *Jaironim* soil, with a Massaporan arrow through your back. My version wins out, you piece of shit. Mine. Not yours."

No one admonished her.

When they returned to Ayyit's cabin in the woods, it was Prala's turn to ask the questions.

"What now? The Harrish have the Funatan stones. Will you try and bring another *Dachahelu* into the world?"

Boselmia took Ayyit's hand. She was the *Fechebolo* now, entrusted with the weight of resurrecting the *Dachahelu* and returning the Massaporan people to his waking dream. And she would. In due time. But not yet. For now, she would keep the Accord. For now, she would let the Harrish fight a different war. For now, she would take a moment for herself, and try to learn how to love.

"One day, Brother, I will finish what our mother started. But that day is not today."

9

199 A.D.

Boselmia found her way back to Ayyit's grave. Her thoughts were a black hole, deeper than death; she supposed the grave of her onetime lover was as good a place as any to give them free run.

"I've lost him," she said to Ayyit. "Can I join you?"

A moony rain came in on flyby, gray-washed clouds. Sporadic raindrops played a not-quite staccato song on the leaves. The cloud cover broke two or three times, sunlight dancing in the limbs. When a swath of sunlight warmed her face, she fell asleep standing up. During this brief interregnum, she dreamed a short dream. In the dream, Jueshwella's fish-pecked face looked up out of Ayyit's grave, saying, "Go away, you've lost him, no one wants you here." Boselmia called for Ayyit, but her lover was gone, departed from her own grave. When she awoke seconds later, the rain was coming down in earnest.

The day's gloom burgeoned. Settled.

She thought that she might stand there forever.

It was then that she saw Doshensa. He was on the far end of the burial ground, his injured body supine on the dirt, teetering next to a grave. Wispy strands of gray smoke danced around him, slowly dissipating.

Doido's son. Losing his grip on the gray lands. Dying, but not yet dead.

She felt an electric stirring. Life. She moved toward Doshensa, weaving around the bone-packed pockets of dirt with a growing urgency. The dark clouds of her concussion momentarily parted. Here was purpose: killing *Koeceti*, killing a direct descendant of Doido Mass. She felt a sudden shot of adrenaline as a perverse thought occurred to her: if she finished off Doshensa, maybe she could dig up his dad's grave, bury father and son together?

"Little Stuck-Shit," she said when she was close. His eyes opened, resigned to his fate. She squatted next to him, brushing away the last of the gray ribbons. One strand curled around her fingers like a baby snake, but its hold was weak; it dissipated like the others in the process.

"Fecheholo," Doshensa replied. He said the word as if it were an honorific. The surprise of it tugged at her heart. She took a moment to study Doshensa. She had known the boy long ago, but only as the son of her enemy; most of what she knew about the man she knew from others. He was a handsomer version of Doido, built of the same materials but more solidly constructed. In his hair he wore two white feathers, an affectation that Doido would have never indulged. She decided that unlike his father, he was no fanatic. He was simply playing the role that his father had made for him.

The shared commonality almost made her feel for him. They both had lived for so long in their parents' shadows.

"You're dying," she told him.

He responded with the smallest of head nods.

Suddenly, the thrill she had felt at the notion of killing the son of Doido Mass left her. She couldn't see how it mattered. The *Dachahelu* was still gone. Ayyit's bones still lay in their grave. Jueshwella's face remained fish-pecked, Prala hung from a Harrish noose, and Maisa resided in *iiwase,* watching Boselmia make a mess of being the *Fecheholo*. Sending yet another *Koeceti* to the grave would bring her no closer to finding peace, or to returning her people to the *Dachahelu's* waking dream.

She looked at Doshensa. There was one thing she could do, however. Something that she had never done before.

She could show him mercy.

"Lie still," she told him. The *jwonatuwe* stirred in her blood, the old familiar energy, creation and destruction competing for her attention. She reached for the magic, thinking at first that she would usher Doshensa into *iiwase* on a pain-free cloud, but then, as the *jwonatuwe* surged to the surface, she was struck by the impulse to save his life. The thought of it was so radical that it made her laugh. Laughing witch that she was, she brought her hand out to cast her spell, the laughter rising in her because she couldn't believe what she was doing—she was going to save Doshensa of the *Koeceti*. Why? She had the strange feeling that this was what Notel would want her to do: it was the message the little *Dachahelu* had been trying to send to her before he ran away. How could she not have seen it? He was a god of love, not a god of war.

And she could be the same thing.

Doshensa's right arm was next to the grave. She reached for his left. As she did this, his right arm slowly came to life, reaching across his body to meet her arm on its descent. They grasped each other's arms at the same time.

She poured the *jwonatuwe* into him on the back of a winged healing-word. His body quickly came to life, restored by her gift. His grip strengthened as his power returned to him; he held on to her arm with a passion that was equal parts bewilderment and gratitude.

She gave him a smile, perhaps the first genuine smile she had given anyone since Ayyit had died.

He smiled back at her, his eyes settling, cooling. Then he took a deep breath, letting his eyes close.

When he opened them again, she saw that something had changed.

Doshensa, son of Doido Mass, spoke a word.

The floods rushed in.

Cast of Characters

Boselmia – The Raven Queen (in Massaporan, the *Fecheholo*)

Notel – The Deer King (in Massaporan, the *Dachahelu*)

Maisa – The Raven Queen before Boselmia, Boselmia's mother

Wolfresh – Massaporan Chieftain, founder of the modern Massaporan nation of Wolfresh

Doido Mass – Nephew of Wolfresh, also known as Cloudworm

Doshensa – Doido's son, one of the seven *Koeceti*

Prala – Boselmia's half-brother (executed by Harrish settlers in Haven)

Hasol – Minor Massaporan chieftain

Ayyit – Boselmia's lover in her old age

Cayap – Minor Massaporan chieftain in the north, father of Shayo, Boselmia's daughter

Jueshwella – Cayap's wife, Boselmia's lover for a time when she was younger

Shayo – Boselmia's daughter

Hiata Oxaway – Effanarem Chieftain, founder of the modern Effanarem nation of Oxaway

Daniel Redgrave – Olgard ambassador to the indigenous nations of Wolfresh and Oxaway

Brigand and Mathias Potter – Identical Twins; Brigand killed the 4th Deer King, Yestric

Etu – One of the seven *Koeceti*

Aagili – One of the seven *Koeceti*

Ash – Keebro priest

Jaan – Boselmia's friend when she was a girl

Deities referenced in *The Sundering*

The Raven Queen (Fecheholo in Massaporan)

The first Raven Queen was born or created before the onset of time, and died sometime after the death of the first reincarnation of the Deer King

Bo – Born 368 B.D. Died 297 B.D.

Maisa – Born 106 A.D. Died 176 A.D.

Boselmia – Born 128 A.D. Died 199 A.D.

The Deer King (Dachahelu in Massaporan)

The first Deer King was born or created before the onset of time, and died at the hands of Funato, the Rain God

Notel – the 2nd Deer King, or, the first reincarnation of the Deer King

Ahuszill – the 3rd Deer King, aka The Deer King who ruled

Yestric – the 4th Deer King

Riiyisti – the 5th Deer King

Notel – the 6th Deer King

Funato

A Jindois god also known as the Rain God, still worshipped by the Effanarem and Keebro peoples.

Author's Note

In the next novella, we're headed to Olgard. After our close-ups of life in Wolfresh (and, to a lesser degree, Haven) we're going to delve into the heart of Harrish country, where an idealistic young man is struggling to come to grips with his place in a country that espouses the democratic ideals he so cherishes, but fails time and again to live up to them. Along the way, he's destined to cross paths with our heroine from novella one. It's time to see what Emmaline Rain has been up to...